T HE LAST OF THE RAMSAYS

"I wake up every day hoping that Thomas never comes back from the Crusade." Elenor's lower jaw stuck out as she looked away.

"Elenor," said Father Gregory gently, "you are betrothed—promised. There are duties that go beyond what we each want for ourselves."

"It was our fathers who wanted this. Not Thomas. Not me. It was a conspiracy of papas."

Father Gregory closed his eyes to better find a reply. "It is the responsibility of parents to arrange good marriages for their children. Noble marriages must benefit all of the villagers and peasants who depend on the lord. You and Thomas are each the last of your line."

"I *know*." Elenor burst out, "I love my life! It's not my fault I'm the last of the Ramsays. Even if Thomas has changed, I don't want to have his children. I will die, like my mother did. . . . " Tears filled her eyes and rolled down her cheeks.

FRANCES TEMPLE

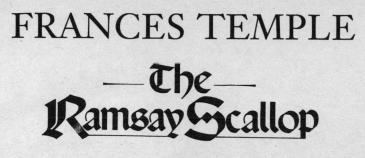

HarperTrophy
A Division of HarperCollins*Publishers*

Acknowledgments

Thanks to Jose Luis de Celis for the mackerel story, to Teresa Gonzales for the old woman with the skull, to Maria Fatima do Minho for talk of calvaries.

Thanks to Burke Wilkinson and Maureen Flynn for historical advice, and to Robin Smith, Cynthia DeFelice, Jimmie Bevill, Frederick and Lindsay Nolting for their enthusiasm for a rough manuscript.

Thanks to Chaucer for giving us "Griselda and the Loathely Lady," to the sculptors and painters of the pilgrim way and to Lindsay, who helped me see their work, to Pierre Maury, who spoke to a tribunal in 1320, and to the scholars who pass his words on to us (*Montaillou, The Promised Land of Error* by E. L. Ladurie, Random House, 1979), to David Macaulay for his book *Cathedral* (Houghton Mifflin, 1973).

Thanks to Dick Jackson for threshing these sheaves with energy and goodwill, and to Maggie Herold, Linda Cabasin, and Janet Pascal for patient winnowing.

Thanks to Tyler for sheep-watching, Jessie for adventuring, and C.T. for companionship all along the way.

‡ v ‡

A Note on Languages

Differences between French, Spanish, and Italian were less pronounced in 1300 than they are today, although there were more variants of each: langue d'oc, Navarrois, Castellan, et cetera. A person who knew Latin, as most educated people and clergy did, could communicate all along the pilgrim trail.

English, with its Saxon and Germanic roots, stood apart, though the Normans had brought many Latin and French words into the mix. Elenor and Thomas speak English at Ramsay. Both were taught French as children, since it was still the language of the English nobility at that time. At the time of this story, Thomas is fluent in French, the lingua franca of Crusaders. Elenor has had less practice.

Contents

For
ANNA BROOKE
who left home early
and came back strong

Elenor

Elenor clutched her too-long cloak around her, wrapping her fingers in its edges to keep them warm, and stood on tiptoe in her borrowed shoes. The sound that filled her ears was so piercing and sustained it seemed to be coming from inside her head. She wanted to make sure it wasn't.

Between the shoulders of the crowd, Elenor caught a glimpse of a beggar-musician, a mangy cat perched near his head. Crouching, she wriggled her way past bellies and elbows. The sound grew louder. Yes, it was the man's hurdy-gurdy, badly rosined, and its screech was devilish. The man's eyes glittered, hypnotic as a snake's, as he cranked.

"It's a sin," Elenor heard one matron whisper to another.

"Not natural," the other muttered, shaking her head, transfixed.

The man's dog crouched on a stool in front of

him. His cat sprang onto the dog's back and turned in slow reluctant circles, its whiskers quivering. Its fur stuck out, tense and uneven. As the punishing sound of the hurdy-gurdy rose higher, a mouse scampered from the beggar's hand and skittered up the leg of the dog and onto the cat's back, where it cowered, trembling.

Do something, Elenor told herself.

A sudden commotion broke out at the cheese stall nearby. The beggar stopped his playing for a second, craning his neck with the curious crowd. Elenor stuck out a toe and jostled the stool. She jumped back, delighted, as cat, mouse, and dog sprang in opposite directions and disappeared among people's legs. She backed quickly into the thick of the crowd, stamping her feet to warm them.

Four times now, Carla had let Elenor make the long walk into Peterborough market with Father Gregory. This time was best of all: Michaelmas, last festival of the year before Advent, in the last year of the century, 1299. Excitement and fear were in the wind.

"We're all trying to be good this year," Father Gregory had told her, "to impress God."

"In case it's the end of the world?" she had asked, expecting reassurance.

"That's right."

She wished he had added "but don't worry." He hadn't.

She tried to imagine the end of the world. Even the end of Peterborough market. What would happen to all these boisterous, jostling people? The big stone Peterborough Cathedral, newly built? The pink-cheeked child just now dragging his mother toward the food stalls? The barrows of carrots and onions and turnips, the pig snouts and limp bunches of chickens, the cooks imagining winter stews, the farmers hoping to trade for wooly socks? The beggars, musicians, tumblers . . . could they just disappear?

At the end of the world came Judgment Day. How could people be judged, when each was as full of surprises as a king cake? She, Elenor, was not yet fourteen, still freckled and wild haired, just starting out; she had no idea what might be in her of good or evil. . . . She tucked the fear of judgment a little deeper. Peterborough market was a rare treat, a rare adventure. Tomorrow she would worry about the end of the world.

A rickety wooden stage stood lashed to the portico of the cathedral.

"Which guild is giving us the play?" Elenor asked a farmwife selling chickens nearby.

"Weavers," the woman answered. "They'll make us forget the cold." She grinned at the girl, showing long, yellow teeth. Then she narrowed her eyes, pointing at her with her nose.

"Ain't you the little lady from out at Ramsay castle, the one that's to marry Lord Thomas, him that's away so long in the Holy Land?"

Elenor managed a nod, but she pulled her cloak tight around her again and turned away to cut the conversation short. Let the woman mind her own chickens.

Elenor caught a whiff of roasting chestnuts. A sooty girl was stoking coals under a pan. Closing her eyes, Elenor could feel the heat of the coals on her cheeks, her eyelids glowing. She untied a halfpenny from the corner of her shawl and pressed the coin into the girl's hand, reaching past the smaller children who hovered near the heat. The vendor scooped hot chestnuts into Elenor's shawl, and she hugged them against herself so that the warmth shot through her vest. She scanned the bleachers, saw Father Gregory, and careful not to lose her shoes, climbed toward him.

The old priest, sitting on the top board, lifted his head. He held open the side of his cape for her, and she crept in.

They peeled the chestnuts, munching the sweet white meat, scattering the hot shells. The sun shone bravely but the wind blew cold. The makeshift curtains on the stage billowed and flapped, and

Elenor glimpsed frantic preparations backstage. Farmwives in homespun and blue caught at their market-day coifs, yanking them back into place and tucking in wisps of hair.

Three loud thuds and the play began. Two child jesters in tights and tunics pulled back the curtains, shimmied up the side supports to tie them, slid down, ran to center stage where they bowed in every direction, and in high, shrill voices proclaimed:

> *"Welcome, welcome*
> *One and all*
> *To the story of Adam*
> *And his fall."*

Then the jesters stared at each other, bowed deeply, and hurried offstage.

Elenor leaned her elbows on her knees and her chin in her hands.

The stage was decorated with plants and branches to represent the Garden of Eden. Beneath it, red devils draped against the stage supports writhed and groaned, chanting monotonously:

> *"Eternal remorse, eternal remorse*
> *The song of the damned is eternal remorse. . . ."*

High above, perched on the edge of the bell tower, an angel tried to look serene while pieces of his wings blew away with the last of the leaves into the fierce blue autumn sky.

Adam and Eve stood midstage under a painted apple tree. Serpent, painted with scales, oozed from behind the tree, offered Eve an apple, and as she refused, followed her around the Garden. With slithery, enticing gestures, Serpent persuaded Eve to accept the fruit. Eve took one bite, danced with delight, clapped her hands, patted her stomach . . .

Elenor narrowed her eyes, shutting out everything but the stage, seeing the scene before her as a painting. The tree separated the stage into halves now, Serpent and Eve on one side, Adam, alone and forlorn, on the other.

Eve reached out a hand to Adam, offering him the apple; Adam stepped across the stage to Serpent's side, took the apple, and bit it. A shout of glee went up from the devils. From heaven, an angel waved a golden sword at Adam and Eve. Wailing, they fled the Garden.

Elenor sighed and rubbed her eyes. "I knew it," she remarked, as the curtains closed. But what remained in her mind was the tilt of Eve's wrist as she held out the apple to Adam, and the kicked-dog curve of Adam's back as he and Eve slunk from the Garden.

When the curtains opened again, plants and

branches were gone. The middle stage, between heaven and hell, was strewn with rocks. Two brothers, Cain and Abel, bent side by side, planting. They stretched tall to quarrel, shouted, and fell to fighting. In the heat of anger, Cain took a rock and bashed Abel. Abel stiffened and crashed to the ground. He bucked, writhed, and died. Cain froze, his arms held high, his face distorted by horror.

The avenging angel bore down on Cain, chasing him away.

Elenor watched Cain's huddled form leave the stage and make its way, limping and hurrying, through the audience. Some of the crowd booed him as he passed.

Moved and somehow angry, Elenor wiped away tears with the flat of her hands. She hated Eve, with her combination of womanly wiles and dissatisfaction. She hated Eve for wanting more than she had. But Elenor was curious, too. She would have tasted the apple, just to know ...

"Why did God punish Cain?" she asked. "The moment he saw Abel was dead, Cain was desolate."

Father Gregory opened one eye. "Expiation," he said.

"What is that?" asked Elenor. "I forget."

"Expiation," Gregory repeated. "It means that he needed to put the sin outside himself, to get away from it. Cain wandered the face of the earth until he walked away his anger and his shame."

"Just walking can do that?"

"So they say," Gregory said.

"Let's walk, then," said Elenor restlessly.

2

Ramsay

Saint Nicholas' Day. Christmas. Feast of the Holy Innocents. Day after day of cold rain on snow.

"What we have to do," Elenor told the younger children, tired of being kept inside, "is be mummers. Kill the winter, bring on the spring."

They scattered, shouting, through the empty halls of Ramsay castle, looking for costumes. Elenor smeared her face with carmine paste. She pestered Carla, the cook, to find the milk goat's horns, cut off last summer. She stuck these through her hair net and tied them to her head. She stuffed a pillow under her cape at the back of her neck and came limping out as Beelzebub, the devil.

Spring came to Ramsay, and Elenor climbed into the wild plum trees, hiding among the blossoms. All of the children felt the pinch of hunger as winter supplies ran out.

"Out, sparrows! No more cringing round the fire," said Carla, shooing them from the castle kitchen. "Find us some greens. A barley cake for the one that brings in most!"

The children fanned out in search of the dandelion and crécy greens that dotted the brookside in dark clumps. Elenor dumped one muddy apronful after another on Carla's table and ran out for more.

Hedges flowered between the fields. Elenor gathered wildflowers, weaving them into garlands, and watched as farmers plowed open the earth and planted oats on the ridges. Then, with the village women and the other children, she was allowed to fill her apron with beans, take a furrow, and plant a long, careful row, tamping the cold dirt with her bare feet.

When Father Gregory rang the bell for lauds, the sun was already coming up, and farmers left their warm beds, threw open shutters, fed dogs, milked cows, and headed for the fields. When he rang tierce, people in the fields were sweaty, thirsting for a drink of milk or beer. When vespers sounded the time to trudge home, the sun still shone, obliquely painting the furrows of earth dark red, the hedge shadows copper, and the sheep pink.

At night Elenor, settled by the kitchen hearth,

sketched lambs in charcoal, overpainting them with beet juice.

Seven times every day, Father Gregory rang the bells of Ramsay church, which served Ramsay castle and village and the far-flung manor of Thornham as well. On the morning of Easter of the year 1300, the dawning of the new year and the new century, he rang them longer and louder than he ever had before. His shoulders ached and his callused hands blistered, but still he pulled and pulled on the heavy ropes. Sometimes the weight of the swinging bells lifted him off the ground, sandals flapping, and he felt like shouting. The world had not ended! Life had never smelled so green, so new, so fine. All his people were alive. Half had gone to the hills with Friar Paul, sick with dread of Judgment Day. The other half had chased their fear by carousing around a bonfire, and this morning lay dead drunk among the haystacks, beaten and disheveled, while the ashes of the bonfire smoked forlornly. Gregory had watched the revelry from the churchyard above, hearing just enough to make him grateful for darkness and distance. Bad enough that he should have to spend this beautiful morning in the confessional.

Flying on the bell rope, Gregory felt a tugging

at his robe and opened his eyes to see Elenor laughing up at him. She jumped from one foot to the other, hair uncombed, nose and cheeks red from running in the early morning. She helped the priest pry his clawed hands from the rope and dragged him out into the sunshine.

"Look!" She pointed. On one side of the valley, wending down from the hills, came a procession of people in gray, their heads covered. Wisps of mournful song floated across the fields.

"Welcome, you dismal Doomsdayers!" Elenor shouted through cupped hands. "Sun's up!" She pointed at the eastern sky and danced a jig. Father Gregory hoped Friar Paul and the penitents were too far away to notice as Elenor, singing loudly, tucked her arm through his and tried to drag him into a dance. His ears were still ringing and he felt altogether dizzy.

"Quiet, child! Don't mock them," he said sharply, collapsing on the stone bench that ran along the outside wall of the church. Elenor flopped beside him, leaned against the old gray stones, and gazed out across the valley. One of the figures in the hayfield stirred and rolled over: A man clad only in a rust-colored shirt crawled to the ditch and retched. The sound carried in the still air.

Elenor smiled; then a shadow crossed her face. "Are those my choices out there, Father? Join some brute in a haystack, or else become a nun and"—she rolled her eyes heavenward—"look to the world beyond?"

A glance at Father Gregory made her quickly add, "Oh, sorry, I love the Church, Father. I do. But suppose I went into a nunnery and the nuns were Doomsdayers, like Friar Paul? Dread, guilt, and *miserere* for my whole life. . . ."

"I'm not offended," said the priest. "You'd rather drink new wine like that fellow down there, dance jigs, bear hordes of children to play with you in the hay—"

Elenor heaved a great sigh, cutting him short.

"The children, yes, I'd like to have children," she said slowly. "But the getting of them, Father, I fear as much as I fear the quietness of the Church." These words were said humbly, like her confessions, which Father Gregory had been hearing since she was a small child. The priest spoke carefully.

"You are betrothed to Thornham's Thomas, who is no brute as I remember him. True, he has been gone for eight years, and may have changed, but as a lad he was—lively, but kind."

"He locked me in the henhouse. I screamed until my eyes were popping out, Father, and between every scream I could hear him and his friends laughing at me."

"He used to tease you because it embarrassed

him to be betrothed to a child, and himself only fourteen years old."

Elenor was not mollified. "Bullies don't change. I wake up every day hoping that Thomas never comes back from Crusade." Her lower jaw stuck out as she looked away, across the valley.

"Elenor," said Father Gregory gently, "you are betrothed—promised. There are duties that go beyond what we each want for ourselves."

"It was our fathers who wanted Thornham joined with Ramsay again. Not Thomas. Not me. It was a conspiracy of papas."

Father Gregory closed his eyes to better find a reply. Elenor had been sold, but what good would it do to remind her of it? More precisely, her wardship had been bought by Robert of Thornham, Thomas' father. Robert was a hard man, and ambitious, and when Guerrard of Ramsay was dying, unable to raise the yearly scutage due to their overlord, Robert had paid the tax for Ramsay, thereby extending his lordship over Ramsay's lands. Robert had procured a run-down but respected castle, the title of Ramsay, and Elenor for daughter-in-law. A smart move, in which Elenor had no say and which left her no recourse.

The mildness of Gregory's voice did not betray the anger he felt. "It is the responsibility of parents to arrange good marriages for their children. Noble marriages must benefit all of the villagers and peasants who depend on the lord. Ramsay's farmers need Thornham's mills. Thornham's villeins need Ramsay's fields, and Ramsay castle's strong walls in case of attack. Look how the lands join. . . ." He waved a hand over the rolling hills, furrowed now, the village and hedges, the wattle-and-daub houses that straggled along the road leading to Thornham Manor, a few hours' walk away, where Robert of Thornham—Robert of Ramsay now—still lived with his bailiff. "It was all Ramsay once; it is all Ramsay again. You and Thomas are each the last of your line."

"I *know*." Elenor was quiet for a minute, aware of her rudeness, but then she burst out, "I love my life! It's not my fault I'm the last of the Ramsays. Even if Thomas has changed, I don't want to have his children. I will die, like my mother did. . . ."

Father Gregory was appalled to see tears fill her eyes and roll down her cheeks. So many fears for one small, generally cheerful child. And each was real and well-founded: Elenor was too small to bear children easily. Rumor had it that the Crusaders were returning, Thornham's Thomas among them. If he should claim his bride, young as she was, it was more than likely that she would die in childbirth as her mother had.

What could he do? Sir Robert had arranged

everything according to law and custom. The earl of Leicester, Robert's liege lord, was the only person who held any sway over him. Leicester wouldn't listen to a parish priest. He listened to vassals who paid up, listened only to armed force and money.

If Thomas didn't come back, it would be still worse for Elenor: Sir Robert would marry her himself.

And what of Thomas? Gregory remembered small kindnesses, it was true, like the time all the boys had knocked down a beaver dam, and young Thomas had caught all the baby beavers and put them safely in a new home. But he also remembered Thomas as a big youth, his shaggy dark hair hanging in his eyes, his face flushed with enthusiasm for killing the Infidel. He remembered his voice booming in the courtyard, the crack of sticks and bones as he beat the other boys in practice fights one after another, his big hands on the staff sure and strong and heavy. Gregory remembered that Thomas had not been successful with the beaver kits; they had all died one by one.

Elenor wiped tears off her cheeks with dirty hands. "Father? I'm sorry to blubber. It's just— may I ask you a covetous question?"

"You may try. What do you covet?"

"My neighbor's life, I think."

"Whose life do you covet?"

"Oh! Elise's. Maude's. Carla's, even. Elise isn't betrothed. She can marry anyone she wants. She can work as a cobbler and never marry."

Father Gregory took his time thinking. Elenor helped a ladybug crawl onto her hand and around her fingers. Finally he said, "Elise may marry only with her father's consent and that of her father's lord, Sir Robert. Carla is a cheerful worker, but she must work hard all her life in the kitchen of another, and then go home and take leftovers to her own children. When she is too old to work, she will live on the charity of her children and neighbors, and will feel bound to do as they say."

The ladybug flew from Elenor's hand. "I'm still envious, Father. Some people do have choices. Men, especially. When Thomas of Thornham was the age I am now, he went galloping off across the world!" She kicked a stone, hard; it skipped and rolled down the hillside.

Father Gregory rose slowly to his feet. He bent over the flower borders of the church, pulling weeds, pinching dead blossoms off the irises. Elenor joined the work. She began talking again, half to herself.

"Friar Paul says that women are to be kept inside and should pray more than men, because they are evil. He says that if it hadn't been for Eve, we would all still be in the Garden of Eden. Do you think that women are wicked?"

Father Gregory pulled up a stalk of grass and chewed on it.

"Everybody I've ever talked to feels wicked some of the time."

"In the confessional . . ."

Father Gregory nodded. "All these people . . ." A rare grin crept across his face. He stretched one hand toward the field where the revelers snored. "Those people invite good and chase meanness by enjoying their bodies and getting drunk." He pointed toward Friar Paul's procession, dispersing now in front of the castle. "Those over yonder, whom you so rudely call Doomsdayers, try to chase the evil in themselves with the scourge, and starve out the devil with fasting, so that God will come into them."

Elenor studied Father Gregory. "You love them all?"

"Yes," he said.

"Though they hate each other?"

"Sometimes they do."

"But are the men just as bad as the women?"

"Just as bad." His eyes twinkled under bushy brows. "Probably worse." He wiped the garden dirt off his hands and onto his robe. "Let's leave tomorrow's worries to tomorrow. Thomas isn't home. Soon you will be fourteen, and you are every day growing taller and stronger. I need to hear the confessions of our brothers and sisters in the hay, who will soon be crawling this way. You go to the kitchen and help prepare a good meal for our brothers and sisters of the hills." He fixed her with a stern, pale stare, his eyebrows curling wildly in the morning light.

"Our brothers and sisters," Elenor repeated.

"They have been fasting and praying all night, Ellie, and not just for themselves. For us all, and for the new century."

Elenor listened quietly, her head slightly tilted, sizing up the intent of his words.

"Don't call them Doomsdayers, Ellie. They would rather be called Penitents."

"Yes, Father," said Elenor. "I'll go help Carla make porridge for the Penitents."

"Do that."

She smiled suddenly and dropped him a curtsy. She ran from the churchyard, heading for the castle kitchen.

3

Thomas

It was Billy the scullion's turn to do the marketing in Peterborough, and he nearly killed himself running home to Ramsay with the news he heard there. The Crusaders had landed. Their ship had docked in Dover, and they were headed home. Thirteen men from the county came on foot, six on horseback. Thomas of Thornham led them, looking, rumor had it, like a hero.

The castle kitchen was thrown open to the village and fires burned all night. Morning found Elenor chopping garlic and onions with Helen. Tears streamed down her face and she shrugged her shoulder to wipe them away with her upper sleeve, not wanting to touch her garlic-drenched hands to her eyes. Carla was up to her elbows in flour, kneading dough with Maude and Elise, yelling at Billy to bring in more wood.

Almost all of the women who filled the kitchen had men who had gone out eight years ago. Some had taken other men since. Some, as Elenor thought about it now, had borne several children since their husbands had left. Helen and Elise, Elenor's boon companions, had grown up in a village where men were few and women had learned to do men's work. Elise had become the village cobbler. Helen looked after the pigs and helped Carla with the butchering.

Billy, just twelve, red in the face as he sat in front of the fire turning the spit to cook the roast, bore the brunt of the women's apprehension.

"So you're not going to be the only man around here, Billy! You're going to have to start brushing your hair."

"Stand back, folks. No telling what varmints will crawl out."

"Be sure to warn us first, Billy-o."

The conversation drifted to jokes about weddings and beddings, the laughter nervous. One of the women urged Elenor to leave the kitchen. "Wash the dough off your elbows and get ready to receive that big handsome knight of yours."

Elenor's skin crawled, and Carla said, "Stay with us awhile, Ellie. There'll be time enough for dressing up if they slept last night in Norwich, as Billy says."

"And if Billy has made up the whole thing—"

"Just to get us to prepare him a feast...."

* * *

The last thing Elenor wanted to do was to leave the warm, busy kitchen and go up to the solar, which she had once shared with her parents.

She had loved it there when she was little. Back then the castle had been gaudy with banners and tapestries, loud with shouts and music and the clatter of hooves. But her mother had died trying to give birth to a sister, her father had died of illness, and now the solar was just a big empty room, waiting for something to happen. It was hers, but she had no idea how to fill it.

Since her sixth year, Elenor's family had been all of Ramsay. Ramsay's peasants welcomed her at their fires and in their yards. Only a very few old people singled her out by calling her "Lady." It made Elenor feel lonely when they did.

When Carla finally told her to go on up and change clothes, she took Elise with her to the solar. They found some of Elenor's mother's dresses in a chest, some they'd used for play costumes. They shook them out, trying to smooth the velvet. Elenor stepped into a long dress and hitched it over a belt so that it would clear the floor. The dress had a musty smell and made her nose run. Since she had no mirror except a beaten brass plate in which her face swam dimly, she had to rely on Elise's word that she looked "like a *real* lady."

*D*ogs barked in the courtyard. Children shouted, shrill with excitement, and Father Gregory's voice called up the stairs to the solar. Elenor came down reluctantly and stood by him at the top of the courtyard steps. Her face was clammy cold. She stretched her neck, trying to feel tall and independent. Her neck felt as thin and vulnerable as a martyr's.

Women crowded out from the kitchen, waving aprons. Chickens squawked; horses whinnied. Elenor clutched her elbows and bit her lip. The men clattered into the courtyard.

They were ragged, but they rode or walked as if on parade. They were, Elenor saw, as anxious as the women. Not sure if they wanted their adventure to be over; not sure of their welcome after so many miles.

Seeing their discomfort broke Elenor from her misery. She ran down the stairs and called out the words Father Gregory had told her she should say.

"Welcome, men of Ramsay and Thornham, and welcome, Lord Thomas. Billy and the boys will see to the horses. There's bathing as always in the river, and feasting on the green when you are ready."

Father Gregory smiled at the way the words were shouted, like Olly-Olly-in-Come-Free, above the noise of the courtyard. He wanted to cheer for

Elenor. He watched as Thomas, a huge block of a man now, got slowly off his horse and bowed over Elenor's hand. He watched Elenor shrink.

At dinner Elenor threw bones to the dogs and looked at Thomas from the corner of her eye. Thomas ate and endured, and looked often to his men, as if for reassurance. Father Gregory kept a thin line of conversation going. Eight years stood impenetrable between them.

After wine was poured all around, a shout went up from Thomas' men.

"To the fair Lady Elenor!"

Elenor, white-faced and startled, quickly glanced at Thomas, meeting his eye for the first time. "They've been toasting you all the way home," he said.

"Me? Why me?" She bit her tongue. She realized why. To them she was an ideal, like a lady on a tapestry. Thomas was the picture of a lord. She must be the picture of a lady. She returned the toast shakily, but swallowing the wine was beyond her. When no one was looking, she spit it back into the cup.

Father Gregory's confessional was teeming. Those who had finished confessing their sins came out from behind the brown curtain reluctantly, blinking in the light, stumbling past people waiting for the good Father's absolution. Thomas strode by the church several times, glancing in quickly, pretending some other errand. When at last he saw that the booth was empty, he slipped in.

"Forgive me, Father, for I have sinned...."

Afterward, he went to the stables. He saddled up Daisy and rode out into the hills, away from the castle and village, exploring half-remembered paths. He murmured to his horse as he rode. He had bought Daisy in France on his way home and had been getting her used to his voice and his mind. "I think, if we go up here, we will find a creek.... Right! Here we are, finest water in England.... Would you like to drink, then? Let's go closer. Watch out, mud's soft here...." As the horse drank, Thomas watched the sun playing on the water.

He had been dreading this homecoming. Self-loathing had kept him from planning what he should do to make it a success. He did not especially want to marry the Brat, a skinny, contentious child playacting at being a lady. He did not especially want to rule Thornham, much less the greater lands of Ramsay. From all reports, Sir Robert was doing that job better than he would ever do it, seeing that land within his jurisdiction was well apportioned and cultivated, and all taxes collected. And there was some struggle brewing between two religious factions. . . . Thomas dreaded most of all going on to see his father, but he couldn't put it off any longer.

When Thomas thought of his father, what came to mind was a long-ago birthday, Thomas' sixth. His father had just given him a short sword. As Sir Robert buckled it around his son, he had explained in his precise way, "There are three states of humankind to which a person may belong. Listen, and remember this.

"The first estate is the clergy; it comprises the priests and nuns who pray for our souls and keep all people in the way of salvation. The clergy includes the monastic clergy like Friar Paul and the secular clergy like Father Gregory.

"The third and lowest estate is the peasantry, whose task is to work the land and feed all of the people. Peasants are weak by nature and must be governed, kept in the way of justice, and protected from natural disasters and invaders.

"The second and finest estate is the nobility, to which you were born. The duty of a noble is to protect all the people and to administer justice."

The word "protect" had kindled in Thomas the hope of a dragon, and he had asked, "How, sir, how should we protect the people? Where is the enemy?"

Sir Robert, who always had an answer, had said, "For some years now, no enemy has attacked us here at Thornham. But there are still many enemies in the world. The worst are the enemies of Christianity, the heathen Moors who try to tear the world away from God."

Thomas grew up learning the skills of a fighting man, and all the while he had pictured the enemy as a dark-faced Moor. Tilting down the field toward a post with a helmet on it, he would shout, "Take that, Muhammad!" and knock off the imaginary enemy's head. Fighting with some towheaded farm boy, he would mutter, "Die, Saracen," as he cornered his adversary and drove him to the ground.

Confessing to Father Gregory had made him remember what they'd done. People here at Ramsay still called it a Crusade. As if Thomas had gone straight to the Holy Land and crossed swords with Saladin himself. As if he, Thomas of Thornham, shining with the light of righteousness, had dealt a blow to evil, some wicked, swarthy heathen.

Crusade. War in the name of a cross.

I was taken in, thought Thomas, stunned by his own stupidity, *stupid sheep that I am.*

And here I am, back in the hills of home, quaint as a prayer-book painting. No job. No wife. If Ramsay were a painting, I would rip it to shreds, throw it in the fire.

The thought brought a sort of backwash in Thomas: he loved Ramsay—its impatient people, its stubbly fields.

Let people believe I'm a hero. They won't think it for long. Let them enjoy the fairy tales in their own minds.

I'm the one who is bad.

He stared at the bright green grass poking up through the dark mud at the creekside.

Grass and mud are real. Grass and mud are beautiful. I should throw my body back into the earth, snuff out my own badness. Make the Ramsay grass grow greener.

At first, the Crusade had been everything he had hoped for. After a joyful gallop across France, Thomas' little band had joined knights of many nations who had answered the call of the Pope. They lived for excitement, encounters with new people, languages, ideas.

They lived by their swords. And there was no organization, no idea as to how these fighting men should be used.

"Turn back," they were told. "The Crusades are over. Acre, our last bastion in the Holy Land, has fallen."

"Wait," they were told. "The Pope wants a new Crusade. True Christians will not accept defeat."

"But King Louis is dead."

"Yes, and so is Saladin."

"The Muslims have never been stronger."

"Is that a reason to quit?"

"Wait. Believe. Be ready. You will be needed."

They were drawn into political skirmishes by petty kings. They became mercenaries because they had to eat, hired killers trying to believe in the causes of those who paid them. Some pillaged and stole in the name of God. Some became involved in the blood wars against the Albigensians, killing at the command of the Church entire families who held a different view of Christianity from that of the bishops. Many became drunkards in their shame— violent, armed drunkards.

One night, in a dream, Thomas had found himself galloping down the tilting field at home, aiming his lance at the "Moor's head" that always stood on a post at the far end. He galloped faster and faster, in wild excitement. He steadied his arm and knew triumphantly that he would hit the head straight on. At the last moment, he saw that the Moor's head had his father's face. He galloped on, awash in the anticipation of victory.

There was a crash and he woke up. As he lay trembling and sweating after this dream, he saw that he had gone on Crusade to knock his father down a peg, and he despised himself.

He had taken months to gather those who had come with him from England, to persuade them to head home.

Something about the shape of the rocks he was staring at reminded Thomas that there was a pool nearby, a little upstream. He patted Daisy's neck and she lifted her head, turning her ears to his tired voice. "Let's go look for a swimming hole, old girl." They turned upstream and headed along the creek until they found the pool, deep and lovely as Thomas remembered it. Leaving Daisy to eat grass, he stripped and swam in the icy water.

He had gone to Father Gregory hoping for a stiff penance and absolution, hoping against reason to wipe the slate clean, to be able to start new. As he had answered the priest's questions, everything he could remember doing seemed done for the wrong purpose: to please his father, to vex his father, to escape. It would not be possible to go back far enough to start over. He should have known. The priest had promised penance in a few days and sent him off with only a blessing.

Thomas rubbed down with cold gravel, took one last dive, and dried himself with his shirt. Then he dressed and cantered toward Thornham Manor, to face his father.

4

Gregory

Father Gregory knelt on the cold stone floor of his room until he decided the familiar pain in his knees was distracting him from the more useful pain of his thoughts. He got up and stared absently out of the window across the kitchen garden, heartsick with the confessions he had heard. How he wished he could just mumble a formula and pass them on to God like unopened packages. But no. He, Gregory, was cursed with the need to seek solutions on this earth.

None of Ramsay's families who had been separated for eight years was truly together again. How could they be? The returned Crusaders, who confessed blithely to murder, theft, and rape, were resentful of the changes in their wives and children. The women, try as they might to make the men's homecoming joyful, were afraid of the changes in their husbands and of a coldness in themselves. They had all learned too well to get along without each other.

Then there was Friar Paul, gleefully stoking the fires of discontent. Under the guise of offering a prayer at the end of the homecoming feast, the friar had cursed the women who had taken other husbands, calling their children the "offspring of Satan." Luckily, thought Gregory, few of the children had heard, as they were mostly off playing leapfrog and looking at the new horses.

Gregory shook himself. What of Thornham's Thomas? His big, square fingers, locked through the grille of the confessional, had squeezed the wood so hard they had turned white. His face, what Gregory could see of it, had been streaked with tears. Yet his voice had stayed flat throughout the long confession. It was the voice of hopelessness, almost of madness.

And what of Elenor? Would her joy be lost on Thomas, sucked down in the quicksand of the poor man's disillusion? The fear of it was like an aching in Father Gregory's chest, so strong that he slipped back onto his knees.

"Speak through me, God. Forgive them; help them forgive themselves. Give them strength to help each other. *Kyrie eleison*, Lord have mercy upon us."

* * *

Long before dawn, Father Gregory woke with an idea so startling he sat bolt upright. When Carla stumbled downstairs to light the breakfast fires, she was amazed to find the priest had brought in wood for her, done the milking for Billy, and was hoeing up a new vegetable plot with the energy of a man possessed.

"A good morning to you, Father Greg!" she shouted. "Have you come upon the fountain of youth?"

Father Gregory kept on working, humming to himself, trying to slow his mind enough to think about the idea that had come to him.

After three days of riding the estate behind Sir Robert, three days in which he felt increasingly unwanted and alone, Thomas came back to Ramsay to receive his penance. Father Gregory asked Elenor to join them in the chapel. They knelt, a few feet apart, awkwardly waiting to see what he could possibly have to say to them together. Each wished for a moment to speak to the priest alone, but Father Gregory was unusually formal and impassive. His words echoed off the stone walls like the binding vows of a sacrament, and for one horrible moment, Elenor thought he had called them there to be done with it, to marry them on the spot.

"Would you, Thomas, and you, Elenor, be willing to do penance for this whole community?"

Each said yes, first Thomas, then Elenor, a puzzled frown on her face.

"Would you be willing to put aside considerations of your own happiness if it would restore the people of all Ramsay to spiritual health?"

Again they both nodded, Elenor's lips framing a silent question.

Father Gregory took a deep breath, like a man about to dive off a high cliff. Elenor and Thomas both leaned forward on their knees, ready to catch him, and then straightened, embarrassed.

"The penance I impose on you, for the sake of the entire community, is to bear a record of our sins and contrition to the shrine of Saint James in Spain, to lay it upon the altar of the cathedral in Santiago, and to pray there for us all.

"You will travel as chaste companions.

"Your marriage may not be consummated until the pilgrimage has been completed."

For a moment they continued to kneel before the old man in the small stone chapel, Elenor so astounded she felt her heart stop. Then they were both on their feet: Elenor, elated, incredulous, hugging the priest; Thomas still wearing the solemn expression he had assumed to receive his penance, because he wasn't sure how he felt.

❊ ❊ ❊

Elenor burst into the kitchen and announced the news. Helen shrieked. Maude threw a ladle in the air. Carla gave Elenor a hug that lifted her off her feet, then burst into sobs.

"One of us, one of our very own, taking up the scallop shell!" whispered Maude, awestruck.

"What scallop shell?" asked Elenor.

"The scallop shell you wear on your hat, when you've made the pilgrimage to Santiago," Helen explained.

"What hat?"

"Your big black hat. It goes with your staff and your gourd, so everybody knows you're a pilgrim," said Helen, miming every word. Elenor covered her face with both hands, feeling very, very ignorant. The smaller children clustered around her now, pulling on her dress and asking questions.

"Is it far, Ellie?"

"Will you be home tomorrow?"

"Will you bring me a yellow bird?"

"Can I come?"

"Father Greg! There you are!" she heard Carla's voice say. "Come in here by the fire, and tell us a story. These little field mice need to learn about where our Ellie is going."

* * *

Maude stoked the fire and called in Billy. Carla shouted for Thomas, but he was nowhere to be found. Elenor sat on the floor across from Father Gregory, her back against Carla's knees. A dog put its head in her lap. Children sat all around the priest, while Helen went quietly about her chopping, listening.

Gregory leaned back, the warm firelight playing on his face. He put a hand on one child, then another.

"The story begins in Galilee. A land of milk and honey, a land of fish and pomegranates, a land where . . ." His voice trailed off and he looked at a child for prompting.

"Where Jesus grew up."

"Yes. Jesus was a boy in Galilee. He worked as a carpenter, but he also fished. His uncle Zebedee was a fisherman on the Sea of Galilee, and his cousins, James and John, were fishermen, too.

"Cousin James was loud, and strong, the best swimmer of them all. By the time he was, oh, fifteen, he could stand balancing in Zebedee's boat and pull in the net, heavy with fish, a smile on his face.

"When Jesus began to teach in the farms and villages around the Sea of Galilee, James and John were both grown men, but they left their work to walk with him, gave their catch to feed his followers. And Zebedee was old, but he helped, too, letting people sleep in his house when it rained.

"So you can imagine how they all felt when Jesus was crucified. James was so sad and so angry he knew he had to do more than just fish. If he couldn't have Jesus alive by his side, he could keep his ideas alive. James remembered the things Jesus used to say, and repeated them to everyone he met.

"James had a booming voice, and people listened to him. After a while, he made his way down to the Mediterranean Sea and talked to sailors there. A ship's captain gave James free passage all the way to Spain, on the other side of the sea. In Spain, Rome had colonies much like Judea, places where people fished and farmed and tended vineyards. James preached there. He started some small churches. Then he boarded a ship and sailed back to Judea.

"When James reached Judea, Herod was king." Father Gregory paused in his story, picked up the poker, and stirred the fire. "Remember Herod?" he asked the children.

"He's the king who killed all the babies because he thought they might be the Messiah?"

"Yes. The old Herod was crazy, fearful for his

power, and the new Herod was just as cruel. All over his kingdom, there were people calling themselves Christians, preaching, drawing crowds, setting up churches. When Herod found out that James, Jesus' cousin, was back from Spain, he sent some soldiers and—you know what they did. . . ." Gregory looked around at all the upturned faces and slowly put his hands around his neck.

"They chopped his head off."

The children squirmed uncomfortably and the dogs looked up in interest.

"You think this is the end of James' story? Well, it's not," said Gregory, resting his elbows on his knees.

"After the execution, a ship made all of stone put in at Jaffa, manned by knights, none of whom spoke a word. The knights scooped up James' body and sailed away.

"The ship of stone sailed across the Mediterranean and into the great ocean beyond the Pillars of Hercules. In seven days it reached the west coast of Spain. It stopped in an inlet between rocky cliffs. This inlet was a holy place, the doorstep of a pagan priestess who had the power of early blades of grass in her fingertips. When the priestess saw the ship, she turned her face to the night sky and howled. Wild bulls came down from the mountain, and pushed the ship to a burial ground called Compost-ela, the field of stars. The knights covered the ship with earth and disappeared."

Elenor noticed mouths were hanging open and closed her own. Compostela. A shiver ran down her back.

"Do you think that's the end of the story?"

Several children shook their heads. Gregory leaned forward, his fingertips touching.

"Have you heard of the Moors?"

Again children nodded, and several crossed their arms over their chests.

"The Moors came to Spain from Africa some five hundred years ago, under the banner of the Prophet Muhammad, and in place after place, throughout Spain, people left their churches and began to worship Allah in the mosques of the Moors. The Moors were such mighty fighters, and the fear of them was so great, that soon the only people who were still Christian in Spain were those in the very north, in the mountainous regions, and those in the part near the sea where the pagan queen had reigned. One evening some of the last Christian soldiers were camping up in the mountains, huddled in a cave, almost ready to give up.

"It was then, so they say, that a bright star appeared to them. They followed it to Compostela, and there they found the ship that was the tomb of

Saint James, shining in the night. They built a church around it. They prayed and found courage. At their next battle, they were led by a vision of Saint James riding before them on a white horse. They won the battle, and many more, and because they did, Spain is Christian again, as James set out to make it so long ago."

"Is that a true story?" Billy asked.

"What do you think?" Father Gregory asked. There was a long silence. At last Elenor spoke up.

"James the fisherman was true. . . ." The listeners nodded all around. "And maybe the pagan priestess and the wild bulls." Nods and head-shakings. "And I think the rest of it was made up."

"By me?" Father Gregory asked.

"No!" said all the children.

"By the soldiers?" said one.

"I don't know," Gregory said. "Why would they have made it up?"

"So they could fight better?" said Billy.

"Maybe so," Gregory said.

"Why do people still go there?" asked Maude. "Why is Ellie going there?"

"It's a good place to pray," said Father Gregory. "It has always been a good place to pray. Even in the days of the pagan queen."

5

The Sending

C an you ride?" asked Thomas, surprising Elenor in the stable.

"Can a duck swim?" she muttered. *He doesn't remember me at all,* she thought. *I've been riding since I could walk. He probably doesn't even remember the horses.*

"This is Clovis," she said, rubbing the bony back of the old workhorse. Thomas pulled a turnip from his pocket and Clovis chomped it carefully from his palm, slobbering. *His hands are as big as plates,* thought Elenor, watching with disgusted interest as Thomas cleaned them on a bundle of straw.

"Clovis was young when I left."

"He's been working harder than you, then," said Elenor, meaning to be funny, but glad to be mean.

Thomas was quiet, stroking Clovis. "He's been more useful," he said, and moved to the next stall.

Elenor followed him, feeling vaguely ashamed of herself. "This is Mab, sweetest horse in the world."

Running her hand over Mab's glossy flank, Elenor had a sudden urge to show off. "She runs like a Michaelmas wind. Watch."

She led Mab out of her stall and talked to her a minute in low tones. Then, sinking her hands in the mare's mane, she jumped astride bareback and galloped off, hearing behind her a sound that was almost a laugh. When Thomas caught up with her, riding on Daisy, she looked at him with her chin in the air.

"Daisy is glad she won't have to carry us both across the Pyrenees," Thomas said.

Elenor didn't ask what the Pyrenees were. She would ask Father Gregory.

Hold this for me." Father Gregory handed Thomas a bunch of smoking rags. "Wave it at any bees you see headed our way." Deftly, the priest sliced honeycomb away from the straw shell, placing it in chunks on a big wooden trencher. A few bees droned ominously; Thomas flapped the rags, turning them so that they would catch the breeze, smoulder, and smoke. Father Gregory extracted honey, the thin first flow of spring. Thomas watched, distracted from his troubles.

Father Gregory carefully put the hive back in place, picked up his knife, and set it on the edge of the trencher.

Thomas followed the priest into his house, and Father Gregory poured him a mug of ale and took one for himself before he spoke.

"I trust you found Sir Robert well?"

Thomas nodded and rubbed his big hands on his knees. He seemed very ill at ease.

"Does he need you, Thomas?" asked Father Gregory. *Where was the man?* he wondered. *Not answering a direct question.* "Do you think Sir Robert can manage the estate without you?"

"Of course," said Thomas, remembering all too well what his father had said, and the dismissive tone of his voice. *"I hope you understand, Thomas, that you'll be Lord of Ramsay in title only. It has been arranged with Leicester that the actual governance will remain with me."*

"But you are troubled, I believe," Gregory stated, wary of prying. "Will you make this pilgrimage wholeheartedly, Thomas?"

"Why are you sending me, Father?" Thomas burst out. "Was it my father's idea? Did you arrange it with him?"

"No," said Gregory. He looked at Thomas over the edge of his mug, then set it down and smiled. "To be truthful, Thomas, the whole scheme came to me in my sleep. I want to attribute it to the Holy Spirit, but that may be brash of me."

Thomas rose and walked to the window, where he stood with his back to the light. Father Gregory could see the bulk of him, but not his expression.

"Why a pilgrimage, Father? Isn't it still another way of running away?"

"Pilgrimage can heal the soul, Thomas."

"If riding down dusty roads were good for the soul, I'd be a holy angel, Father."

Father Gregory sighed. "You don't believe the people here will be helped by sending their sins to Saint James?"

Thomas drank his ale and gazed out the doorway. He understood very little of the rift between the Penitents and others at Ramsay. But he thought about the men he had traveled with, about the sins they had bragged of and the sins they hid. He nodded grudgingly.

"They might."

"Then do it for them, Thomas."

A bee flew in, looking for the hive-robber, and settled on the rim of Gregory's mug.

"There's another reason I want you to go, Thomas, and it's this. You've a good head on your shoulders, and Ramsay will need you soon enough. But right now, people here need forgiveness more, forgiveness and the feeling of a new beginning.

"While you and Elenor are seeking forgiveness

for Ramsay, I want you to be readying yourselves for the work you'll have to do when you get back here."

"You think there'll be—changes?" Father Gregory heard a ring of interest in Thomas' voice for the first time.

"I think that the days when the peasants really needed the lords to protect them are over. It seems to me that the peasants could take care of themselves if they didn't have to feed the nobles, too. I think there are things a lord can do, should do, to earn his keep, besides fight and collect taxes. Sir Robert isn't doing a bad job, according to his lights, but he, or you, could do better."

Thomas moved back to the table and sat down across from Gregory, looking into his mug and swishing its contents in a circle. "There are more of us knights wandering over Europe than there are fleas on a dog. We've forsaken our code. We're turning into bandits, Father. I've become ashamed of what we are."

Father Gregory flicked a bee off his arm.

"Then the time has come to change, Thomas. The road is one place you can find out about change. Talk to people: see how governance works in other places, and what responsible lords are doing with their serfs and holdings. If you see any good ideas at work, it wouldn't hurt to talk them over with Ellie."

Thomas rose, taking his mug to the bucket to rinse it. "Elenor's too young," he said.

"Youth is no sin," said Father Gregory. "She has ideas worth listening to."

Won't we be home by winter?" Elenor asked. No one knew.

Elise made each pilgrim a pair of stout sandals. Carla knitted thick wool socks, "just in case."

Maude sewed clothes following Father Gregory's instructions: "Tough, ugly, and good for all weather." Divided skirts, both alike, dark brown. Like Thomas, Elenor also had two plain linen shirts, a heavy cloak, and a wide-brimmed hat.

"Tell me I don't look like a mushroom in this hat," she begged Helen.

"You don't look like a mushroom in your hat," Helen said, too quickly, and then threw her apron over her face, so that Elenor could see that her fingers were crossed.

There was horse talk. They chose the two best: Daisy and Mab.

"Can I take paints?" asked Elenor. "I'll see so much."

"No," said Gregory.

"Can I take her?" she asked again, showing Father Gregory a rag doll Carla had made her years ago.

"No," said Gregory.

Thomas tried slipping some fishing gear into his pack.

"No!" Father Gregory said, pulling out net and hooks and dropping them on the ground.

At mass he preached that the proper way to go on pilgrimage was with nothing, only the spirit and those minimal necessities that keep body and soul together.

"Pilgrimage is painful," he said, looking fiercely at the Penitents in the congregation. "Painful and hard. How else can it pay for our sins?"

Father Gregory drew a map. They were to cross the channel at Yarmouth, then ride east across France to join the stream of pilgrims going south from Paris. Friar Paul, rhapsodic, called the stream of pilgrims "a great cleansing river, the lifeblood of the Church, flowing always to and from Santiago, the heart of Christendom."

"Friar Paul, blood and gall," Elenor chanted to Helen very softly. "Lord Thomas looks like he is about to throw up in his hat."

Saint Mark's was the day chosen for their departure. All Ramsay, Thornham, too, rose to the ringing of matins. Farmers, children, dogs, people carrying their sick and their babies, all gathered in darkness and lit smoky torches to see the pilgrims to the bridge.

The horses pranced a little, so that Elenor and Thomas had to rein them in tightly. All around them, people walked. Billy played hymns on his flute; another boy beat a drum. Sir Robert rode at the back of the procession, deep in conversation with Friar Paul. Father Gregory walked at the front, between two torchbearers, intoning the hymns with his eyes half-closed.

To Elenor everyone looked too serious, even the children, still pale from sleep. She stared at each one, suddenly realizing she was leaving them, trying to hold pictures in her mind to take with her. Mostly she saw the browns and grays and purples of the countryside before dawn, wisps of ground fog and smoke, and the tops of people's heads.

When they got to the bridge, Thomas and Elenor dismounted. Everyone knelt on the dewy grass while first Friar Paul and then Father Gregory gave his blessing. Father Gregory had inscribed the prayers and confessions of the people on parchment and sealed them in a leather pouch. He entrusted this pouch to Elenor in words that rang out over the kneeling people.

"You, Elenor, lay at the feet of Saint James the confessions of our people, their resolve to walk in the ways of the Lord and to serve him through honest living and honest toil. Receive for us absolution, so that we may forget the sins and troubles of the past and live boldly as children of God. Go in peace."

"Amen!" roared the crowd—Carla, Maude, Billy, and all the rest.

Elise and Helen boosted Elenor onto Mab; hands clung a moment to her foot and skirt. Then Thomas and Elenor rode across the bridge into a silent misty calm broken only by birdsong as the sun hit the first high branches of the trees.

6

Bird of the East

I *would be so happy,* Elenor thought, *if only I were in good company.* She tilted her face up to the sun that dappled the trees. Mab skittered along the road at dancing gait. Elenor chose ideal companions: Helen, Elise. Maybe Billy.

Elenor tried to stay well ahead of Thomas. *He rides as if pilgrimage were a chore,* she thought. *Killjoy.*

They rode through marshlands and mucklands, scaring up flocks of ducks. Close to Walney Cross they met pilgrims on their way to the local shrine. Some were in drab like themselves, some decked out in colors with tin saints sewn on their clothes and caps; some pranced on horseback, some hobbled on foot dragging palsied limbs. Elenor wanted a friend to share it with. Overwhelmed with homesickness, she felt she might burst into tears.

Thomas was thinking of Gregory. *It's a small task the priest has handed me,* he thought, *simply to get to Compostela and back again to Ramsay. I can do it badly or well, and it won't much matter to anyone but me.* Relief made his bones soft. He felt safer hiding emotion behind a stony face.

He must remember that he was not alone. He should try to talk. In the last months people had become unreal to him. Again, the priest had set up the simplest challenge: he needed only to get along with Elenor.

The Brat, thought Thomas, *was wily as a rabbit, alert as a grasshopper with its antennae out.* It was no use to pretend with her; she would know a mask. And he had no idea how to make her happy. She always seemed to wish he were someone else.

A cluster of pilgrims on horseback was laughing uproariously just ahead of Elenor. She nudged Mab closer. The center of attention was a strapping gray-haired fellow who threw back his head at intervals, laughing from deep inside at his own story. Elenor was enchanted. Every time he laughed, she laughed, scarcely listening to the words, noticing only that his story had many mentions of "swiving" in it, whatever that was.

Thomas rode up beside her and laid a hand on Mab's reins. "Let's fall back and let these pilgrims ride ahead."

Elenor snatched the reins from under his hand. "I'll ride where I please," she said stiffly, "and hear the end of the story."

Thomas looked somewhere past her ear. "Such stories—" he said.

Elenor was suddenly furious. "What's it to *you*, sir? I could use a good laugh after riding all day with a Moor's head!"

She rode off through the crowd with her back very straight. Gradually the words of the gray-haired man's story came through to her and she felt a flush creep up her neck. She longed to do what she and Helen might have done, to throw her apron over her head. Now that she was supposed to be a pilgrim, she didn't have an apron. And she didn't have Helen.

After Walney, they found themselves traveling alone again, in awkward silence. A woman came toward them loaded with brooms.

"Pretty brooms you have," said Elenor, by way of greeting.

"Going to Moddsbury?" the woman countered. "Fair's on, but folks aren't buying."

A fair, Elenor thought. *Other people. Thank God.*

As the crowd thickened, they dismounted and led the horses. Elenor was glad of a chance to stretch. Thomas bought winter apples, and tossed one to her. As she bit into it, Elenor caught him eyeing her warily, and looked quickly away.

Moddsbury Center. The fair clustered around two big elms. On a rope stretched between the two trees, a woman balanced, swung, danced, her big callused feet on a level with Elenor's face. So sure and strong. Elenor wished for paper and charcoal.

A barker shouted above the noise of people, challenging the men to a contest of strength. Beside him a barrel stood, attached by two ropes to a pulley and a stout leather handle.

"Come one, come all! I am here to announce that *anyone*, that is to say any one person, be he short or tall, fat or thin, *anyone* strong enough to lift this butt of malmsey into this wagon here will win a fabulous prize—an exotic bird of the East, ready to sing for you day and night!"

The barker's furtive eyes scanned the crowd. "Just one halfpenny will buy you a chance to win this beautiful bird for your girl. You there, pilgrim!" he called, catching sight of Thomas. "That black hat wasn't made to hide under!"

These words brought laughs from the crowd, and people turned toward them.

"Come on up here, and let's see if a pilgrim can do anything besides pray!"

"Want a bird?" Thomas asked suddenly. Elenor

almost looked behind her to see who he was talking to. Out of sheer surprise she raised her eyebrows and nodded. Thomas handed her Daisy's reins and stepped forward.

The crowd cheered when Thomas threw off his hat. A man next to Elenor swung a child up onto his shoulders for a better view. Elenor found a wheelbarrow to stand on, looped an arm over Mab's neck, and held Daisy's reins loosely.

She saw the barker exchange winks with another man. Thomas looked ridiculous, large and ill at ease. He also looked as if he could lift the barrel of wine easily, even without the pulley. But carnival barkers were high on the list of villains Carla had warned her about: "Slick as the devil's shoe," she'd said.

Thomas handed over his halfpenny and the barker gave him a leather glove. Thomas put it on, grasped the rope handle, and leaned into the rope, seeking by feel the moment when the barrel would catch his weight and rise. It didn't. The barrel felt like part of the earth it sat on. He leaned until his whole weight hung from the pulley. Nothing budged.

The crowd's admiration changed to laughs and taunts. Thomas was being made a clown. The barker, behind Thomas' back, rolled his eyes at Thomas' efforts, encouraging the crowd to laugh.

Thomas struggled with the rope, then threw it off his hand in disgust. He tackled the barrel directly, laying his face flat against it, the cords of his neck bulging out, his hands grasping the ends of the barrel. Sweat poured off him and his shirt clung to his back. Laughter died away. The crowd held its breath. Slowly Thomas lifted the barrel off the ground about waist high, and staggered under its weight. Then he threw it down and it cracked, spilling stones.

A growl rose from the crowd. Someone spat at the barker, and Elenor saw fists clenched and lifted. The man swiftly reached inside his wagon and drew out a big bird wrapped in a cloth. He pressed it against Thomas' chest, turning the attention of the crowd, calling on them to cheer the champion. Thomas swung his cape back around him and hurried queasily through the crowd, clutching the bird like a thief.

Elenor watched, her mouth slightly open, a ringing in her ears. She heard the admiring comments of the women around her with embarrassment, awe, and a tiny flicker of the pride of ownership. She was fascinated and repelled by the intensity of Thomas' efforts, by the sweat and bulging muscles. She was curious: would he burst his heart and die?

When it was over, she stood stock-still on the wheelbarrow, and watched Thomas leave. Just before she lost him from sight, she jumped on Mab and, leading Daisy, rode after him. She caught up with him on the road out beyond Moddsbury.

She slid off her horse. "Where's my bird?" she asked, out of breath. Thomas turned around. *His face is pale as a mushroom,* Elenor thought. His scowl lifted. He raised an eyebrow.

"Fabulous bird," he said, winded, his voice rusty, the bird held mysteriously behind his back.

The bird let out a loud *quonk*. Thomas offered it to Elenor and she gently unwrapped it. Out popped the angry head of a duck, just like the thousands that were building their nests on every tussock of the marshes.

"Bird of the East!" said Elenor, in the tone in which irreverent people said "Mother of God!" Elenor and Thomas looked at each other.

"We'll have to take her home," Elenor said.

"Bird," Thomas asked the duck, "where's home?" The duck struggled a little, and then settled under Thomas' elbow, her neck draped over his forearm. He stroked her neck feathers absentmindedly and started walking again. The back end of the duck was very dirty, and so was Thomas. He turned around again, his face red now. "That was stupid," he said, half to himself. "I never should have done that."

"Hey," said Elenor, feeling momentarily as if she

were talking to a friend, "for a bird like this ..."
Then her legs almost buckled under her from surprise. The Moor's head had spoken to her, and she
to him. She stroked Mab's face, tied the reins in
a loose knot, and walked down the road beside
Thomas.

The sun was low now, the sky pink, and the
land looked black except where patches of marsh
water reflected the sky. On one of these patches a
flock of ducks milled softly, leaving dark ripples
behind them, quacking to one another and standing
on their heads for fish.

"Is this home?" Thomas whispered down his
arm. Bird waggled its tail, squirming to get away.
Thomas lifted the duck high above his head and
launched her out over the water. The other ducks
looked up. Bird swam bravely toward them across
the sunset waters. The ducks closed ranks around
her.

Elenor sighed in relief. "That old crook! Bird of
the East—" She thought about it. "East of Moddsbury, maybe?"

Thomas nodded, picking feathers from his
clothes, and lapsed back into silence.

They rode hard all the next day, as if in some
great hurry, morning to evening. The air
changed, grew fresh and salty, and suddenly over

the next green hill was nothing but water, stretching right out to the edge of the sky. The horses stopped, with nostrils flared. Elenor caught her breath, astounded by emptiness.

"Where is France?" she asked, and immediately felt stupid.

"Straight across," said Thomas. "Two days' sailing, with this wind. Don't worry. It looks calm enough."

Not true, thought Elenor. The sea looked cold and treacherous, each little wave pink on one side from the sunset, steely gray on the other, sharp as a knife blade. Why did Thomas never call her by name?

They rode down into town and separated. Thomas went to the wharf to book their passage and look for lodging, taking the horses. Elenor felt conspicuous in her pilgrim garb. A woman and a child passed her, the child turning to stare. She wandered the length of the wobbly wharf and looked at the only ship tied there; *Lady Elwyse* was the name carved on the shabby hull. A mouse made its way along one of the mooring ropes, creeping from ship to shore.

"Turn around, little mouse. Don't you want to go to France?" she pleaded. The mouse hopped onto the wharf and scuttled for cover.

Hungry, Elenor walked back down the wharf

and pushed open the door of an inn. A fire smoked at one end of a low room. The floor was slippery with spilled beer. A woman who seemed to own the place grabbed her by the arm and shook her head at the men who turned to look at her.

"I'll show you your lodging; it's paid for," she said, and led Elenor back into the murk. One of the men blew his nose on the tablecloth as they passed. Up a stair, across a rickety walkway, and into a windowless room with grease-coated walls. Elenor could make out a straw tick lying on the floor. She thanked the landlady, grateful only to be rid of her. Her stomach growled and complained with hunger. Where was Thomas? She went to the door, but hearing snickers of laughter from below, she didn't have the courage to go down. She wrapped herself in her cloak and lay down on the mattress. *Why did I ever think I didn't want to be a baby? I am a baby! It's all I want to be. . . .* Dreaming of warm milk, hugging her knees to her stomach to still the ache inside, Elenor went to sleep trying not to cry.

She woke in the dark.

"It's almost day out," said Thomas' voice, somewhere close by. "The *Lady Elwyse* sails an hour after sunrise, and we've got to secure the horses."

* * *

The horses balked at going to sea. They rolled
their eyes and pulled against their halters, and
it was all Thomas could do to wrestle one down
the ramp to the hold, while Elenor held the other
on shore and talked soothingly, as if she herself
were an old salt, as if she really believed that the
sea held no perils. When at last the horses were
below, and Thomas with them to keep them calm,
Elenor found herself still repeating the words: "It's
going to be all right. Look at the beautiful sea, the
beautiful blue sea that will carry us to France."

She found a place on deck between a stanchion
and the bow rail, out of the way of the brawny men
who yelled orders at each other and curses at the
passengers.

The mooring lines were cast off and the *Lady
Elwyse* drifted quietly out with the tide. With a
shout the boatswain ordered the sails raised. The
patched, dirty canvas flapped loudly in the wind
and then filled, instantly transformed into pink
clouds drawing them forward. The *Lady Elwyse*
lurched, shuddered, and bent to the wind. The land
crept past.

A headland of white cliffs protected them for a
while, and then they were past it, into the open sea.
The waves jumped much higher, so that the *Lady*

Elwyse bucked and plunged, sending up splashes of white spray that sluiced the deck and soaked the passengers. Elenor's heart thudded against her ribs. She stayed in the bow, drenched, her eyes half-closed, clutching the rail, pretending the ship was a chariot pulled by a wild horse. She dared the waves to jump higher still, to hit the ship harder. She kept her balance, riding the ship, salt spray running off the sides of her face like tears.

Thomas, suddenly remembering his resolve to look out for the Brat, climbed over the frightened, huddled passengers and pulled himself along the rail until he reached the bow. He called out to her but his words were thrown back by the wind, and when he drew close to her he was stopped by her fierce ecstatic face. He wondered what she was thinking. He turned and went below to calm the horses.

7

France

The fields were green, the hills dotted with fat sheep and cows, the sky a high and noble blue. The road flowed smoothly between tall poplars, its even cobbles ringing in a crisp clopping to Mab's hooves.

France is more orderly than home, thought Elenor, surprised.

Thomas noticed the social order, which he had taken for granted in the past. He found it both efficient and galling. The road was eight feet wide. When travelers going one way met travelers going the other, a comparison of rank took place: peasants, no matter how old or feeble, moved off the road in deference to anyone on a horse. The mounted squires or knights passed each other closely with a nod of the head and a tight hand on the reins. Everyone made way for a litter. A litter could be as wide as the road, and only a person of rank would ride in one. On the high road to Paris, each person had his place.

Late in the evening they rode up behind a man who was singing, his head thrown back, his eyes half-closed. His black beard pointed forward; a lute hung low across his back. His horse plodded on patiently, seeming to know the road, and they rode up quietly on either side of him, listening. Much later, Elenor wrote down the words he sang, as best she could remember them:

> *"Beautiful Doette is at her window.*
> *She reads in a book but her heart is far away.*
> *She remembers, she remembers her friend*
> *Who has gone to battle in the Holy Land*
> *And her heart is in mourning.*

> *"A squire at the end of the hall*
> *Has arrived and is unbuckling his satchel.*
> *Beautiful Doette comes downstairs, very pale,*
> *In order to have news, whether good or bad,*
> *And her heart is in mourning.*

> *"Where is the one I have loved so well?*
> *Alas, I cannot hide it from you.*
> *My master is dead; he was killed in combat.*
> *Her heart is in mourning."*

Tears rolled down Elenor's face. Thomas glanced at her. The Brat was strange. She didn't cry with fear at sea in a rickety boat. She didn't cry with pain when Mab stepped on her foot, getting off the ship at Le Havre. She cried for beautiful Doette, who didn't even exist.

The last echoes of the song died away. The singer opened his eyes. "Adam," he said, extending a hand to Thomas. "Troubadour by profession, bound for Paris." A sparkle lit his face. "And you, kind sir?"

"Thomas of Thornham, on pilgrimage."

"The road is my home," Adam said, and looked at Elenor, his eyes resting long and gently on her face. "I see my lady likes the song, 'The Beautiful Doette.' " Adam paused and put a hand over his heart. "The most beautiful songs are songs of sorrow. Without sorrow we would be"— he tapped his chest comfortingly—"weak, very poor."

They rode on together.

"Where do you find songs?" asked Thomas.

"The heart, the soul," Adam responded airily, "not to mention my friends and acquaintances. . . . Students, for instance, at the University of Paris, make up many songs. Come to Paris and we will drink and sing together. You will meet Ruteboeuf,

writer of dirges. I will sing you one, to make my
lady weep again."

Adam cleared his throat and looked at Elenor so
intensely she wanted to gallop off.

> *"What has become of my friends*
> *That I held so close*
> *And loved so well?*
> *They were too lightly sown,*
> *I think the wind has blown them away.*
> *Love is dead."*

But Elenor was cheered by Adam's sad song. She
smiled to think of her friends, Carla, Elise, Helen,
Maude, Father Gregory. They were solidly planted.
No wind would uproot them.

They came to a roadside shrine just as the sun
was sinking.

"Abbeville," said Adam, sweeping his hand
toward a paved side road. "A pilgrim hostelry, one
of the most beautiful in our fair France. Be our
guest." He himself stayed on the high road. "The
friars do not welcome troubadours. I camp alone,
and sing my songs to the moon. But, my dear new
friends, we will meet in Paris."

Adam embraced them each in a jangle of impatient horses, tickling Elenor with his beard.

* * *

The hostelry of Abbeville loomed ahead in the dusk. Turrets surrounded a courtyard. Impatient mooing announced a milking barn. Smoke, the clatter of pans, and bursts of conversation came from what must be the kitchen. In the center, the fine black spire of a chapel was etched against the orange sky.

A groom disappeared with the horses.

"Welcome, pilgrims." A shadowy form, robed and cowled, led Thomas and Elenor up a stairway. Stone columns and arching ceilings formed three halls. One, the Brother told them, was for gentlemen travelers, another for ladies and their attendants. The smell of food drew them into the third, the refectory.

Three ladies, elegantly dressed, sat at one table, and when a servant beckoned her over, Elenor joined them eagerly, while Thomas took a seat at another table. Elenor wolfed down bread and leek soup, then, looking around for a second helping, remembered her manners. "The French can cook," Carla had told her. "See what you can learn from them." Elenor turned to the lady on her left.

"Can you please tell me what spices to use to make such delicious soup?"

There was a moment's wait while the lady delicately licked her fingers and wiped them on the tablecloth, and then she asked, cocking her head to one side, "In England, do ladies concern themselves with the cooking?"

She and the other ladies laughed merrily.

"Well," said Elenor, nettled, "I do."

She tried listening to the table conversation as if she expected to be made part of it.

"Peasants just don't know their place anymore," one of the ladies complained with a dainty sigh. "My squire had to bodily knock a farm woman off the road today. My dear, we had to come to a halt for her! There she stood, in the middle of the road, broad as a house, reeking of onions, and gawked at us without moving—"

"Excuse me," said Elenor, rising. "I need to talk to my horse."

Heart banging, she slipped out of the hall and down the stairway to the main door.

The courtyard was dark. *If Carla were here, she would forbid me to go out alone,* Elenor thought. But she couldn't go back up and she must get used to being alone.

A light was shining from the stable. She did want to curry Mab. If she took long enough, the ladies might be asleep by the time she got back.

No one seemed to be in the stable, though a lantern burned at a low table and some tack was laid out as if someone had been working on it. Elenor picked up a brush and went looking for Mab. A whicker in the shadows told her where she was. Elenor stroked her and talked to her, scratching her back where the saddle had rubbed, running her hands over the horse's legs, glad to feel that the muscles hadn't bunched from too much travel. She brushed, singing quietly to keep up her courage.

"Call up your men, dilly dilly, set them to work,
Some to the cart, dilly dilly, some to the plow.
Some to make hay, dilly dilly, some to cut corn,
While you and I, dilly dilly, keep ourselves warm.

Lavender's blue—"

Mab stiffened suddenly and whinnied. At the same time, heavy hands landed on Elenor's shoulders, pinning her so that she couldn't turn around. Fear and regret stabbed her. A man's voice asked a question, and hands pushed down roughly inside her shirt. She could feel the man's breath on her neck, smelling of garlic and rotten teeth. She stood still and stiff, grasping the brush. If she turned to fight him, it would make the man grab her more tightly. And she didn't want to see his face.

Be still, Mab, she willed intensely: she dropped suddenly to her knees, scampered under Mab's belly, and darted to the door. She scurried across the courtyard and up the stairs to the ladies' chamber, all pounding heart and fast, fast feet.

8

Ambrose

Thomas wished he could be camping with Adam, gathering wood, setting snares, cooking. This hostelry was too big, too cold. Why such fuss for pilgrims? Coming into the refectory, he saw a friar sitting by himself. The friar made room for Thomas.

"Welcome, fellow traveler, sit down, sit down. I am Brother Ambrose, on my way to Amiens."

Thomas liked Brother Ambrose's gentle, unpretentious face.

"I teach a school for boys well to the north of here, and it's been many long years since I left home."

"Amiens is home to you, then?"

"Always, no matter how long I'm away. I want to see my sister, and the lads I went to school with, who are grandfathers now. And I long to see our cathedral, which I hear has grown and flowered."

A boy came by and ladled soup into Thomas' bowl.

"Was the cathedral begun, when you left home?"

The friar leaned forward across the table, his eyes shining in the candlelight. "It was," he said.

"The year I was born they razed the houses in the center of Amiens, our house among them. They drove stakes into the ground, and tied ropes to the stakes. The ropes and stakes made a pattern on the ground as beautiful and intricate as a spider's web. I learned to walk holding to the ropes that formed a pattern for the apse: half circles, one within the other like the colors of a rainbow. When my legs gave out, my sister and I would lie together on the grass, looking at clouds, and she would say, 'This is our cathedral. We are inside our cathedral.' "

Thomas ate his soup, listening to Ambrose.

"Later, in the same place, men dug holes for the foundations, and close to the river others were digging great holes, quarrying stone to put beneath the cathedral."

The friar laughed, lines shooting up from the corners of his eyes. "I remember—it was at some family gathering because all the uncles were there, and some of them were stonecutters, and one was complaining of backaches—I asked why he worked so hard to take stones from one hole and put them in another. All the family laughed at me until my mother picked me up and I could hide my face."

Thomas felt suddenly sad. He had never known his mother, who had escaped from Sir Robert to a convent when he was just a baby. He forced his attention back to Ambrose's story.

"By the time of my third Christmas the holes were as big as dragons' maws, and the men lowered blocks of white limestone and lined them up in rows, like teeth. Then the workers joined them together. We children, lying at the top of the excavation, could see that each stone was carved and fitted, so that there were arches as well as solid bulwarks. Each stone had to be completely level, and as each was hauled into place, my uncle climbed out on top of it, lay across it on his stomach, and dangled his plumb line down into the pit, checking to make sure the entire side was straight and vertical."

"What if it wasn't?" Thomas asked.

"Ah!" said the friar. "Shouts! Groans! The stone lifted out again, recut or replaced. And like as not, one stonecutter lost his job."

Thomas liked the idea of checking the lay of every single stone to make sure it rested perfectly in the earth.

"The stones were so smooth," said Brother Ambrose. "I remember the cool of the new-cut stones against my cheek when I was no taller than a pup."

"You helped."

Brother Ambrose laughed. "Well . . . In the fall my sister and I would muck out barns. We'd take the straw and manure to cover the stonework so it wouldn't crack during the winter."

"Was it tall, then, when you left?"

"Goodness, son. I was sent to be an oblate when I was twelve. By then the columns and buttresses were up more than sixty feet. Like stone trees they were, giant trees of stone."

"Did they sway in the wind?"

"No, thank God!" Brother Ambrose laughed. "But I expect the townspeople all slept more easily once the buttresses were joined to the columns."

Ambrose yawned, and Thomas pushed back his bench.

"May I ask you one more question, Brother?"

Ambrose nodded genially, but tears of sleep stood in his eyes.

"Will you ride with us tomorrow?" Thomas asked.

"With pleasure, my son."

Thomas stretched out on the hostelry cot and was soon deep asleep. He dreamed he was standing on a big flat stone, one he had played ship on as a boy, back at Thornham. In his dream, the stone was being lowered into the ground as the foundation for a great cathedral. He strode up and down on the stone, stamping it to make sure it was solid and firm. Suddenly it lurched like a ship floundering. His knees buckled and he was swept by a nauseous vision of crumbling walls and cracking arches. He flung himself full out on the stone, clinging to its edge, begging and willing it to be still, to be firm.

He woke in a sweat and set himself to endure the empty lingering fear by taking up a chore. He found tallow and slowly rubbed it into his boots to make them waterproof.

E lenor woke at dawn to the cheerful sound of birds, and lay for a minute looking at the delicate tracery of the arched windows, not conscious of where she was. Then she remembered the stable and writhed with embarrassment. A monk stuck a hand holding a bell into the ladies' dormitory and shook it heartily. Elenor pulled her blanket over her head. The other ladies must have jumped up: from under her blanket Elenor heard a merry tinkling of chamber pots. She reached her hands out to conduct.

T here was a high mass in honor of the Feast of the Ascension. In the ornate chapel, Elenor sat in the ladies' choir, a balcony that overlooked the male congregation, the altar, and the priest. Behind the altar, windows of glass veined with lead formed a half shell of light. There was a fancy coldness to it that made Elenor long for the homely chapel at Ramsay, with its columns so stout it had taken three children all holding hands, her and Elise and Helen, to circle one of them. She could see Thomas down below, his hair black and patchy-looking, as if he had combed it with his fingers. He stood beside a bald friar. She could hear their voices above the others, raised with the priest's in the old psalm:

> "Clap your hands, all you peoples;
> Shout to God with the voice of joy....
> For God is King of all the earth:
> Sing praises with understanding!"

She could see their hands clapping vigorously.

After mass, when she got to the courtyard with her bundle, she found Thomas ready with the horses.

Elenor rubbed her nose against Mab's and swung into the saddle. With creak of leather and jangle of stirrups, they were out of the arched gateway of Abbeville. Elenor was glad of it.

Thomas introduced her to Brother Ambrose.

"Will you be full of questions, too? You should have been with us last night."

"I should have," she agreed.

Used to his school full of boys, Brother Ambrose called Elenor and Thomas, collectively, lads. She didn't mind.

‡ 76 ‡

9

Ascension

How do they lift the stones?"

"How are the arches held in place before the keystone is set in?"

"But then, to use a pulley, you'd have to..."

Elenor was surprised to hear Thomas asking questions, to see his face mobile, his hands sketching forms in the air.

"Who plans it all?" Elenor asked at last. "How do they know how the parts will fit together?"

"Ah," said Ambrose. "Decades ago our master builder made drawings and showed them to the bishop, to the council, and the people. The drawings showed how high and wide the nave would be, where the windows would be, how many piers and columns and buttresses would be needed. But— how could drawings tell how it would truly be? A cathedral grows like a plant, like a family. Each worker makes his part as beautiful as it can be and still fit the other pieces. And there is always the unexpected. The master builder blends them into one."

"And the master builder, is he still . . . ?"

"As long as Master Roger still has an ounce of strength, he will be working on the cathedral."

Suddenly Ambrose straightened up, and his sorry nag began to prance. Through the trees, far away across the deep green clover, rose arches not yet fully roofed, giant trees of stone reaching into the blue sky. All around them, houses and sheds clustered like baby chicks around a hen, straw roofs shining in the sun.

Ambrose slid off his horse and fell to his knees. Thomas and Elenor jumped down beside him. Tears ran down the friar's face. When he stood up, he clasped his companions by the shoulders.

"Now to find my sister Mathilde. Come with me."

Newly plowed fields spread out from town in all directions, but no one was working. With mass over, farmers rested in the spring sunshine, exchanging stories and watching those who were wrestling, racing, and fighting with staves. Younger women hiked up their long skirts to get sun on their legs. Older women hid their noses under hats. Babies crawled around and were scolded for eating grass and empty acorn shells.

Brother Ambrose walked bedazed, looking for old acquaintances. Thomas led the horses. Elenor followed behind, anxious for Ambrose, praying he would find his sister alive.

Under an oak tree, two men sat playing draughts, their profiles, their large white ears, their vague expressions nearly alike.

"Good afternoon, brothers," Ambrose greeted them. "Can you direct me to the house of Mathilde, wife of Henri?"

The men looked at each other across the board, then turned simultaneously to look at Ambrose.

"That would be Mathilde from down at well side?" asked one.

"No, now, it wouldn't," said the other. "That Mathilde is married to Pierre the carpenter. He'll be meaning Mathilde of the forest."

"No, Guillaume. Mathilde of the forest was never married to anybody, though she must be a hundred years old."

"Too late now, then."

"Never too late, I say. Consider—"

A third old man who had been sleeping against the tree sat up, lifted his hat, and asked in a querulous voice, "Would that be Henri the vintner or Henri the schoolteacher?"

Ambrose threw up his hands. "Who knows? Tell me about Henri the schoolteacher."

"He doesn't have a wife."

"But he soon will, from what I hear."

"Peace!" said Brother Ambrose. "Who can direct me to the house of Henri the vintner?"

One of the brothers got slowly to his feet, took Brother Ambrose by the arm, and pointed.

"You can see it plainly from here. It's the only vineyard hereabouts, and still too far north, if you ask me. I get my wine elsewhere when I can, from—"

Brother Ambrose thanked him hastily, disengaged his arm, and swung into the saddle.

The vintner's cottage was built of large stones, whitewashed, with a smoke hole in one side of the roof and more stones holding down the roof straw. Chickens pecked around the open door. Brother Ambrose walked up to the door soft as a cat. He was pale. Elenor hung back, biting her nails.

She saw a stout, tall woman with a white kerchief on her head appear in the doorway, wiping her hands on her apron. The woman greeted Brother Ambrose politely, then suddenly threw her arms around his neck, making the chickens jump and squawk.

"Come on up, pilgrim friends! Meet my big sister!"

Mathilde was a grandmother now. "Call me Nana," she told Elenor. "Everyone does."

Jeannot, Mathilde's grandson, ran off to spread the news of Ambrose's homecoming, and soon the cottage was full of family and curious neighbors.

"We'll feast tonight in the town square," everyone told Elenor. "You are lucky to have come today, Ascension Day! We'll play music and dance!"

In the evening they got ready to walk down into town. Elenor was given a jug of wine to carry on her head. Mathilde carried a basket of bread; Jeannot brought a cloth, a candle, and trenchers; and Ambrose and Thomas carried Mathilde's big kitchen table between them. Henri the vintner, a kind-faced man with a bowlegged gait, led the procession, pushing a barrel of wine in a wheelbarrow. All the way down the hillside they were joined by neighbors, each carrying something for the feast, so that by the time they came into the streets of town, Elenor had to fall back with Jeannot, holding her jug with both hands so she wouldn't drop it in the jostling.

The portal of the cathedral was already partly built, some carvings complete, some only roughed out, some niches carved but empty. The setting sun lit the stone so that it glowed above the bustle of setting up tables, greeting friends, sharing out food and wine.

A priest stood on a table to bless the food and the crowd. "This feast honors everyone," he said, waving his arms to include them all. "Christ Jesus, who on this day finished his work on earth; Christ's people, who have worked so long and so well to build this cathedral; and his pilgrims, the restless ones."

Thomas shifted nervously. He hated sermons and wished the priest would be quiet and let them eat. Beside him, Mathilde sighed with contentment and leaned over to whisper in his ear, "Don't you think that this is the most beautiful place in Christendom?"

Thomas nodded politely. The word "Christendom" gave him a profound bellyache, but he liked the colorful crowd, the wine, the dogs. And he liked Mathilde.

"What do you suppose heaven is like?" Mathilde asked Elenor when the blessing was over.

Elenor shrugged, but her eyes sparkled. "I think maybe a big, green field, Jesus in the middle, lots of animals, big tawny ones, small furry ones..."

"What do you think, Thomas?"

Thomas, who was watching Elenor in some surprise, turned toward his host. "Cheers, Henri! Your wine is ..." He waved an approving fist.

Henri clapped him on the back and refilled his cup.

A knot of men were making their way through the crowd to a table of honor in the center of the square. Brother Ambrose leaned toward Elenor.

"Look! There is Roger, the master builder."

In the midst of the burghers she saw a very old man all in black, with a fine profile and a humble smile. This was the man who had seen the cathedral through from its very beginning to its present beauty.

Night fell, and bats came out to swoop and dive among the columns. The food had been enjoyed, the crumbs swept down for dogs and birds, and some of the tables pushed back to make room for dancing.

While the musicians tuned up, Brother Ambrose took Elenor by one hand, Thomas by the other, and introduced them to Master Roger. It was dark now. The old man looked at them searchingly in the torchlight, holding Elenor's hand between his cool, thin, papery ones. She could feel his bones.

"Your cathedral—your work is very beautiful," said Thomas.

"We are all working on a building, of spirit or of stone."

Thomas looked at his feet.

Roger smiled. "I am only lucky enough to see

mine before me every day," he said, patting Elenor's hand.

When they got back to Mathilde's table, her daughters dragged them off to join a round dance, women inside, men outside. The music swirled loud and wild. Elenor kicked her pilgrim sandals under a table. Hands grabbed her by the shoulders and spun her off in new directions; she learned the dance in her feet and didn't want to quit. That night, she stayed with Mathilde's daughter, sharing a bed with many children.

Thomas fell into the company of some cathedral workmen and helped them finish Henri's wine. Sometime in the night, he found himself readjusting the tilt of the cathedral with his left foot.

You're limping," Thomas told Elenor when she found him the next day. "I met a stonefitter, last night. He tried to explain to me how stone can be made to arch overhead, and says he'll show me."

Matthieu waited at the foot of one of the broad piers of stone inside the cathedral. Elenor recognized the stonefitter from last night's dancing. He moved lightly, bouncing on the balls of his feet like a cat ready to spring, with the channeled excitement of someone who loves what he is doing. He greeted Elenor by taking both of her hands in his.

"I checked with Master Roger and he says you

may stay here and watch the work, Elenor. He remembers you, and says only to remind you that stillness and concentration are required." Matthieu's eyes shone. "I assured him you would be as still as a saint of stone, and that I would not keep Thomas too long up above. Will you be well here?"

Tracing designs in the air, Matthieu explained the work. Arches of wood were lashed tightly to the tops of several piers in the shape of the arches of stone that were to come. Carefully cut stones were placed on top of the wooden forms and attached to each other securely both with mortar and with their own weight and fit, so that when they were all in place, none could fall out. Then the wooden forms could be removed and the stone would stay.

The pier beside them held in its core a winding stone staircase that spiraled up one hundred feet to the place where the column began to branch out to form arches. "Today," Matthieu said, pointing straight up, "we will work from the triforium, there."

Matthieu disappeared into the staircase, closely followed by Thomas, and it was many minutes before they reappeared at the top of the pier, so far up that they looked to Elenor like tiny animated dolls. She could hardly tell one from the other. She counted six men on the arch. One of these, to her astonishment, was Master Roger himself, looking as insubstantial as thistledown.

It was dizzying to look straight up for so long. Elenor sat down at the bottom of the pier, leaning her back against the cool stone. She didn't dare walk around for fear of getting in someone's way, but she could see carvings from where she sat. At the top of one column was the gentle face of a cow eating leaves; at the head of another column a horse reared, kicking his hooves. On blocks laid out in a rainbow shape around the periphery of the apse, scenes from the life of Christ were newly carved. The one depicting Ascension Day showed Jesus' disciples in a field looking up open-mouthed at a cloud, into which Jesus' feet were disappearing. She gazed at this scene until she felt she had drawn it into her mind, memorized the astonishment of the disciples, the set of their feet, heavy on the ground.

Elenor was tired. She closed her eyes and listened to the sounds around her, the wind playing about the columns, hammers and chisels at work on stone, the ring of a hammer striking metal, the occasional far-off mooing of cattle.

Closer by, she heard low voices talking. She opened her eyes to see two identical stout men sitting on stones in the middle of the apse. She thought at first that her eyes were playing a trick on her; nevertheless she greeted the men politely, as they were looking at her. Both had sparse, unruly hair, wide red faces, bulging muscles. Elenor imagined them, baby twins in leopard skins, wrestling bears, with a huge mother cheering them on. They sat on two of a line of measured stones waiting to be lifted to the arch. Beside them stood a huge, upright wooden wheel connected to a series of pulleys. Ropes circled these, connected to a wooden platform. The twins watched the workers up above, their mouths slightly open, straining to hear directions. Elenor listened, too.

Finally a thin shout came from above. One of the ropes twitched in three short hops. The stout men rose to their feet, hoisted the first stone in line onto the platform, and secured it with ropes. Then they walked side by side into the giant wheel, where they grabbed a hand bar and leaned forward. As they took one laborious step at a time, the great wheel groaned and turned, slowly at first, a little faster as they gained momentum. The ropes tightened around the pulleys until at last the platform swung free of the ground and began to rise into the air. Up and up it went as the twins trotted below, their hairy backs pouring sweat. Another platform, loaded with counterweight, descended in the place of the first, and when it touched the ground, the twins stopped their running and came out to sit, panting, waiting for the next call.

Elenor watched the tiny forms above. One man, probably Matthieu, had jumped onto the platform and was pushing the stone toward its place in the arch. Four others helped. Thomas stood at a distance, out on the arch. Master Roger stood at the other end of the wooden span, at ease on the sloping wood as high as a rainbow. After adjustments too careful and slow for Elenor to follow from the ground, the stone was fitted into place. She heard a faint shout. The twins rose again to their task, rolled the next stone onto the platform, and ambled with the grace of the very strong into the treadmill. Elenor's eyes followed the stone as it rose in the air up to where the men waited for it.

She saw the platform sway and be steadied into place; she saw Matthieu jump down as before and then saw him jump back up onto the arch. Elenor rose to her feet, craning to see what might be amiss. What she saw, she thought at first, was a black bird diving down through the nave. In the next instant she heard the sound of its landing on the stone floor and realized that it was the body of an old man, and saw it there, frail ankles sticking out from beneath the spread black cape.

There was complete silence in the nave. The twins came out of the wheel and knelt down side by side. Elenor, too, had fallen on her knees, and a faintness was overtaking her. A roaring like the wind filled her ears. The forest of stone piers swayed and danced and finally flipped altogether so that she was flying up through the columns, faster and faster. Faces of rabbits and gnomes and goblins looked out at her in amazement as she flew past; a stone bull stopped chomping on a sheaf of wheat to smile; a serene angel, eyes half-closed, raised a long thin hand in greeting. She was falling upward, spiraling now through shafts of light of every color: the purple of spring iris, the deep chestnut of Mab's coat, the green of moss by the brook at Ramsay, the red of wine with firelight shining through it. With a painful and joyous crack she burst out of the top of the cathedral while below she heard shouts and clapping of hands. She saw the little black boots of Master Roger disappear into a white cloud. She felt herself become a bird and wheel off into the blue sky, rowing with arched wings.

Thomas had been watching Roger give directions about the placing of the stone. He had seen the old man press his hand against his heart, slip off the arch, and disappear. Thomas had run down the dark, narrow winding staircase as quickly as he could, and when he reached the bottom he fell to his knees not only because everyone near the body was kneeling, but because his legs would no longer hold him. It was Matthieu who first noticed Elenor in a crumpled heap, who shook Thomas' shoulder and got him to help carry her away from where a large crowd was now gathering. It was he who slapped her face again and again, who rowed her arms trying to get her color back and her blood flowing. Thomas rubbed her cold hands, and when that didn't work got a bucket of water and splashed it over her. Elenor opened her eyes to see the face of Matthieu, emptied by grief. Not herself yet, she looked him in the eye and mumbled, "Matthieu, Matthieu. All is well." Matthieu held her gaze for a moment, and though her gray eyes were not at all like Roger's faded blue ones, he felt Roger looking out at him.

Elenor yawned suddenly and deeply, and the color began to come back to her face.

10

River

In Mathilde and Henri's vineyard, the grape leaves were just beginning to unfold, like tiny hands reaching for the sun. Thomas, saddling Daisy, noticed how pale the Brat still was, and asked Mathilde if there might be a way to leave the high road for a while, another road toward Paris.

Mathilde considered. "The high road is busy this time of year, but there is a path that follows the old market way and meets up with the river. It's too muddy for carts. There'll be no hostels on that path, nor inns either, but it is a quiet way, and there's good water for the horses."

Thomas looked at Elenor.

"Yes," she whispered, resting her face against Mab.

For two days Elenor and Mab, Thomas and Daisy traveled peacefully and almost wordlessly along the old market road, which met the

Oise River and then followed the river's winding course.

The water was shallow. In most places Elenor could wade without it rising over her knees. One evening they camped on the sandy riverbank under a clump of poplars, where someone had left the ring of a cooking fire. Leaving the horses hobbled, Thomas went swimming while Elenor gathered firewood. He stayed far enough up the river to be out of view, but Elenor, more curious than polite, peeked through the willow branches to see him splashing naked in the water. Kitchen jokes from Ramsay echoed in her mind. She had trouble with the tinder, and got a fire going only just as Thomas came back to the camping place.

"My turn," she said.

Thomas frowned. "Do you plan to take down your hair?" he asked.

"Aye, of course, and give it a wash." She had worn her hair all day in a string bag at her neck, to keep it from tangling in the wind. Thomas was looking at her closely, and she frowned, too, mired in seriousness.

"You know," he said, "I think I could catch a fish in that little net."

Elenor, relieved, shook out her hair and tossed him the net. "I'll tell Father Gregory on you."

"It was you who brought the frivolous thing

along," retorted Thomas. His eyes were lively for a minute, as if he might laugh. Then he glanced away and went to work on a fish trap.

By rigging the hair net between two small sand-bars, using willow twigs to keep it open, Thomas caught a river trout. He cooked it over the fire, and shared out chunks of it on the last of Mathilde's bread.

Rain made tiny hissing sounds in the fire. Thomas found a sapling small enough to bend and pegged the top into the sand. Then he threw his cape over the sapling, and they crawled under its shelter. Elenor was comfortable, hearing the horses shift and snuffle and the river gurgle softly by. She and Thomas smelled of wet wool and wild chives. Thomas ground his teeth in his sleep. She wondered what he was dreaming.

Her own dream was of fish, turning and turning in the fast-flowing water along the river bottom.

Elenor woke up alone and hungry. The sky was clear and high. A lark sang. The road was one long mud puddle. She squelched into the woods to pee, found the horses, and saw Thomas out in the river, checking the trap. He shook his head. "Too bright. They see the net."

They packed and swung into the saddle, chewing

on sticks. As they splashed along a road, they brushed the lacy softness of carrot greens, and Elenor knew that if she felt in the soft cold earth under the plants there would be small new carrots there. She thought of them boiled, warm.

"Thou Shalt Not Steal," she found herself whispering. She imagined herself back in Father Gregory's study, sitting in a shaft of sunlight. The Bible was propped on its own table; she sat on a high carved chair with her feet on a stool because they didn't reach the floor. She loved to run her finger over the bumpy painted letters. Father Gregory had taught her to write by making her copy the Ten Commandments. "Thou Shalt Not Steal." It was her favorite because it was short, and she liked making the letter *S*, curling the ends into snail shells.

Thomas rode up behind her. "Look," he said, his wide face solemn as ever. "I've stolen us some carrots."

11

Paris

aris was the first city Elenor had ever seen at night. All her life she had gone to bed with the sun, except for feasts in her own father's hall so long ago she barely remembered them. Even when they'd gone to Peterborough, Father Gregory had always dragged her home before dark. She was excited by all the people passing by with their faces half-hidden, by the dark alleys where cats prowled. She kept turning around in the street to see in every direction at once. She loved being able to peer into warmly lit windows, so many little stages, instant framed glimpses of family life.

Thomas quietly laid hold of the cowl of her cape to steer her around holes in the street, away from windows. It was a little like having a rambunctious puppy on a lead. *Heel, Brat.* He dropped his hand when she noticed.

They found the square where Adam had said to

meet him, surrounded by tall stone houses all leaning on one another. A fountain gurgled into a water trough. Three old men sat on a bench taking the air.

"Evening," said Thomas. "Will musicians play here tonight?"

One of the men laughed; he had a single tooth, bottom center, like a baby. "Maybe a foreigner would call them musicians!" he wheezed.

"Should I be insulted?" Thomas asked Elenor, or himself.

Thomas talks to me the way he does to Daisy, thought Elenor. It was comforting.

They sat on a hitching block, side by side, waiting patiently. Soon the square filled with strollers. There was a stir of excitement and Adam swept in, surrounded by friends, black velvet capes swinging, bright colored ribbons streaming from their shoulders, many with instruments tucked under their arms. Adam made a show of embracing both Thomas and Elenor. Here, among his exuberant friends, with the crowd calling his attention, his friendliness seemed glossy and wide flung.

A hush fell over the crowd as Adam perched on the rim of the fountain and strummed his lute once. A boy settled at his feet with a drum and bone. Other musicians gathered round, or wandered in the crowd.

The first songs were lost on Elenor, sung in harmonies that swallowed the words. She looked at the clusters of leaves black against the fading sky, at the balconies of the stone houses around the square. On one a small child squatted and listened, dropping chestnut blossoms on people's heads. One of the three old men on the bench drifted off to sleep, his head on the shoulder of his crony, his mouth open. She watched the intricate hand movements of the musicians, the drummer's stance as he rose to his feet and put one foot up on the fountain rim, his relaxed concentration. As it grew darker and more people crowded into the square, they stood to watch and listen—Elenor on a curb, Thomas standing behind her, his hands on her shoulders to keep her from being pushed off balance.

After a long and intricate instrumental, Adam began a solo. He sang it slowly, and Elenor watched his face, trying to follow the words, but also not wanting to meet his eyes, which always looked at her too long.

> "On the steps of the palace
> Is a young girl.
> She has so many who love her
> She doesn't know whom to choose.
> A little cobbler

Is the one preferred.
While he was putting on her shoe
He asked her:
My beautiful, if you wanted
We would sleep together
In a big square bed
Covered with white cloth.
At the four corners of the bed
Are four bouquets of lavender.
In the middle of the bed
The river is deep.
All the horses of the King
Could drink there together
And we would sleep there
Until the end of time."

The song left Elenor feeling as if she were in a dream, a stick swirling in floodwaters. To be herself again, she wanted to run away yelling. Instead, she leaned back against Thomas, who crossed his arms around her shoulders. She could feel his heart beating, skipping like the drummer's bone. The growing crowd pushed them together. Thomas rested his chin on top of the Brat's head and resisted an impulse to scratch her scalp.

Early the next morning they saddled the horses, settled up with the innkeeper, and made their way to the Tower of Saint James, where pilgrims bound for Santiago gathered and were blessed and sped south. Elenor kept Mab in one corner of the square, afraid her horse would prance and kick someone. From Mab's high back, she examined the faces of the crowd. Some had expressions of piousness borrowed from saints of stone, but most looked like carnival-goers, flushed with excitement and ready to be off. Beside Elenor, a fat man embraced a woman in a low-cut dress; streams of black eye-paint ran down her cheeks. The man had the baggy eyes and red nose of a heavy drinker, but he wore a new brown Franciscan robe.

Many of the pilgrims were so old they must surely die on the way. One ancient man, half-blind, was making his private farewell to the square, gazing at the shafts of sun coming through the chestnut blossoms, running his gnarled hands along the carvings on the tower, resting them on the impatient heads of children. He approached Elenor, who had slid down to stand beside Mab's head, with a faraway smile, his half-closed eyelids so thin they looked blue, and as he laid his hands on her head she said, "I'm coming with you, Father; I, too, am going to Compostela." He didn't seem to hear. "*Benedicite,* blessings, my child," he said, as he moved on.

There was a hullabaloo on one of the side streets, a press of people being pushed out of the way. Four bailiffs marched into the square, escorting six pale men who limped and blinked like newborn puppies. Their skinny shoulders were marked with welts, their legs bruised. Criminals, sent on pilgrimage to clear the prisons. Elenor stared at them, fear thrilling her backbone.

Priests made the rounds, chanting, and clouds of incense mingled with the smoke of cook fires. Nuns and friars, Franciscans in patched brown robes, Dominicans in dark gray—some mounted, some on foot.

Musicians came to pipe them to the edge of Paris. Elenor swung into the saddle to see better, cheered, and waved. Adam was among them.

"We loved the songs last night," she told him as he jostled through the crowd.

"Oh, did we?" Adam teased. "And did Thomas cry, too?" He grabbed Thomas by the back of the neck and the two scuffled in mock battle. A cacophony of pipe music broke out, gradually resolving into a dance tune. The pilgrims fell into step behind the musicians and the priests. Adam walked alongside Elenor, intoning the tunes between jokes and irreverent comments.

Suddenly Adam broke away, snaked his way through the crowd to a group of students, and dragged one of them across to Thomas. He was a young man with white skin and pink cheeks, dark unruly hair, and blue eyes. Dragged by the elbow, mock protesting, he played the clown to Adam's domineering.

When he looked up to shake Thomas' hand, Thomas was surprised by his piercing and intelligent glance and his firm handshake.

"Etienne is a student, a most serious student of great erudition," said Adam. He clasped his hands before his chest, looking at them all benevolently. "My dear friends, I give you each, as a parting gift, good companions for the road!"

Elenor caught Etienne's eye and gave an Adam-like shrug, palms up. Etienne grinned, and patted his heart. They shook hands all around. The music reached a peak of loudness and confusion, and all knelt on the rough road for one last blessing. Still jostling one another as the road narrowed, the pilgrims began moving south.

12

Pipeau

The road south from Paris led through a deep, gloomy forest. The throng of pilgrims, most not yet used to their six-foot walking sticks, advanced like clumsy thugs on the prowl.

"These woods are famous for fierce wild boars," the student, Etienne, told Elenor, baring his teeth cheerfully. "If one attacks, I'm jumping on behind you."

The sky, glimpsed through the thick trees, had gone gray, and as they came out of the forest it began to rain. Word went around that a hostel run by Cluniac monks lay ahead, and that the monks were generous with soup. Elenor shivered. Mab plodded on, subdued. At last they saw the stone enclosure, with granite scallop shells carved over the door as a welcome.

The tables were already crowded; at each end of the refectory a huge caldron steamed. As soon as a pilgrim was through eating, he took his bowl to be dipped and filled for someone else, and went off to one of the dormitories that flanked the refectory.

Elenor squeezed in at a table beside a young woman with two small children and a baby. She offered to hold the baby while the woman ate. It was a personable baby, though wet on the bottom and sharp-heeled. Elenor jollied it by making faces and disappearing behind her hat.

"How can you make a pilgrimage with three children?" she asked the woman. The woman tucked a length of straight brown hair behind her ear, glanced around her, and whispered to Elenor, "I'm not really a pilgrim. This is the only safe way I could think of to travel with the babes. Their Fa's down in Bordeaux, got a job down there, an' we're going to find him." She drank her soup and watched her children with satisfaction as they tore off pieces of bread, sopped them in their bowls, and gobbled them up. The boy was so thin his elbows stuck out like a grasshopper's, but he had lively eyes, and when a pilgrim on the other side of his mother put down a crust of bread absentmindedly, the boy grabbed it and stuffed it in his shirt.

"What's your son's name?" Elenor asked the mother.

"We christened him Bernard, but we call him

Pipeau, on account of his voice is like a little flute. And I'm called Marthe."

"I'm Nora," said Elenor, trying it on for size. She was tired of Elenor—it had a too-queenly ring—and Ellie was a baby name.

"You're not traveling alone, are you, Nora? Even in the pilgrim cape, it's not safe." Elenor shook her head, her mouth full of bread. Taking a lesson from Pipeau, she had tucked a crust in her sash as well.

"I'm traveling with an Englishman. It's a vow for our village in England. The priest sent us to get a pardon for everybody. Ouch!" The baby had wrapped his hand in her hair and was jerking on it with all his might. Marthe untangled him, pulled out her shirt, and put him to her breast.

"What does their father do in Bordeaux?" Elenor asked.

Marthe's face softened. "He's a juggler-musician. Used to work up and down this road entertaining the travelers, but now he's got a steady job, working for the mayor of Bordeaux."

"Is it a big city, Bordeaux?"

"Aye, I should say so. Big enough to need musicians to play the passing of the hours from the balcony of the town hall. Right fine it is, too, with the banners waving. Not like Paris, mind you, but a fine town."

"You've been there, then?"

"No. Jean-Loup told me. He's their Fa."

More pilgrims were elbowing their way into the refectory, shaking the rain off their hoods.

"Time to find a place to sleep," Marthe said to her children.

"Wait a minute, Ma!" answered her son in a high, clear voice. He slipped under the table, collecting fallen crusts.

"How old is he?" asked Elenor.

"Six come Christmas," said his mother. "Don't know what I'd do without him."

The pilgrims spread their cloaks on the rush-covered floor of the dormitory. Gray stone columns arched above their heads. There were fleas under the rushes, Elenor discovered soon after she lay down. To distract herself, she told Pipeau and his sister, Guillemette, a story Carla had once told her, about a boy who traded his cow for three magical beans, and a giant who lived above the clouds and had a hen that laid golden eggs. When she finished, there was silence and she was proud. But a reedy voice came out of the dark.

"May I ride on your horse tomorrow?"

"Shhhhh!" said Guillemette. "You shouldn't ask, Pipeau."

"Each of you can ride for a little while, if your mother agrees," Elenor whispered.

"She won't," said Guillemette.

* * *

The other mounted pilgrims left directly after morning mass and got ahead of the walkers, but Elenor and Thomas waited, so that Pipeau and Guillemette could take turns riding with Elenor on Mab. Thomas halfheartedly invited Marthe to ride with him, baby and all, but she refused.

"I've never been on a horse in my life and I'll not start now."

With Marthe and Etienne on foot, they all traveled at walkers' pace. To make Mab prance, Elenor sang village dance songs from Ramsay.

> "Oats, peas, beans, and barley grow,
> Oats, peas, beans, and barley grow.
> Do you or I or anyone know
> How oats, peas, beans, or barley grow?"

Pipeau and Guillemette watched Elenor and imitated the sounds, chiming in loudly whenever the word "oats" rolled around.

Thomas noticed Etienne admiring Daisy and offered him a turn in the saddle.

"You've a good way with a horse, for a student," he remarked, as Etienne swung up.

"I was raised to be a horseman, Thomas of Thornham. It's just of late I've become a student, and I had to sell my horse and sword to do it." He patted Daisy's neck affectionately.

Thomas lifted Pipeau onto the horse in front of Etienne. "And what would make a person do a thing like that?"

Etienne laughed. "It's more than you'll want to hear."

"Tell," said Elenor and Marthe together.

Etienne bowed, and then took a deep breath.

"In my youth," he said, "I meant to go on Crusade, to lead fighting men against the Infidel. My father trained me well, taught me sword-fighting and wrestling, bought me a horse when I was ten. My mother had other ideas. She taught me to write, to sing, to read in Greek as well as Latin and French. She taught me a love of thoughts. When I was eighteen, word came to us that Bishop Jerome was to preach the Easter mass in Paris. 'Go,' said my father. 'He will preach a Crusade.' 'Go,' said my mother, with her little smile. I went.

"The bishop did preach a Crusade, of sorts. 'Since Christianity is a religion built on faith, on ideals, on the example of a peaceful Christ,' said the bishop, 'should we not give up our weapons and fight Islam with our minds and words instead?' "

Etienne swiveled in the saddle to find Thomas with his blue gaze. Elenor was surprised to see

Thomas motionless for a moment in the road, stopped by Etienne's words.

"That question is with me still," Etienne continued. "I feel that my training was incomplete, that I should go and learn the language of the Infidel, that I should translate the word of God and the thoughts of Christians into Arabic, so that the people of Islam can hear them." He smiled, his face dimpling on both sides. "It pleased my mother that I should become a student."

Thomas ran now, to catch up with Etienne.

"Were you studying Arabic in Paris?" he asked, his hand on Daisy's flank.

"Nobody teaches Arabic in Paris, Thomas, although there are many who know it. If you try to learn, you are treated as a spy and an Infidel. In Paris I studied the sermons of Bernard of Cluny, the arguments of Abelard, the teaching of Thomas Aquinas; texts I would like to put into Arabic. But to learn Arabic, I must go to Spain."

"Carla saw a book once," said Elenor, "a book someone had brought back from Crusade, and she said it was filled with nothing but curlicues and dots."

"That's how they write down ideas," said Etienne.

"Then our words must seem like little boxes to them," Elenor said.

Etienne looked at her suddenly.

"Where will you go to learn Arabic?" she asked.

"Toledo, in southern Spain. Arab and Christian scholars study there together. Jewish scholars, too, all of them working together to translate texts." He looked ahead as if toward the Holy Grail.

High on Mab's back, holding the little girl Guillemette comfortably in front of her, Elenor watched and listened. Etienne gave off energy and goodwill the way a fire gives off heat. If Etienne was eighteen a few years ago, he must be almost as old as Thomas now. This amazed her.

And Thomas, who had seemed staid as a too-finished portrait, was scattering into a series of sketches. She had thought what he loved was weights and pulleys, stone and tools. Now she heard him apply the same dogged questioning to university studies.

"How do you sharpen your skills, without contests?" he asked. "Are there no tournaments?"

Etienne thought. "The disputation, or debate, is the student's tournament, and as hard to train for as a jousting match."

"How does it work?"

"In the first years of study, you learn by heart what the authorities have said. Only when it is clear to your teachers that you understand the thoughts of others are you deemed ready to lead a disputation. You choose a question of philosophy, and present it to the community of scholars. On the day of your disputation, there are no classes. Everyone comes to hear what you have to say, and to ask you their most difficult questions."

"How can you prepare, not knowing what people will ask?"

Etienne raised his eyebrows and bit his lip, nodding. "You must think about, care about every aspect of thought generated by your text and your question, and these are infinite, of course. The intricacies are infinite."

In spite of this—or was it because of this, Elenor wondered—Etienne seemed as happy in his studies as Matthieu was in fitting stone.

Elenor was still scratching when evening drew near, and decided she would rather sleep outside than face the fleas of another hostel. Camping was not as agreeable as it had been on the river. Too many people had gone before. The roadsides smelled of human excrement; windfalls were gathered for firewood almost before they hit the ground. Thomas followed a stream up from the roadway and found an empty grassy spot. Several fires indicated other pilgrim groups nearby, Marthe's among them. Elenor washed in the creek. Thomas, to his surprise, snared a rabbit, and best of all found some fleabane in the woods for Elenor's cloak.

"Off you get, little fleas," she said, holding the heavy cloth of her cloak with both hands and vigorously rubbing the herb into its folds. "We've come a ways together, but now you're on your own." She combed her hair and let it blow around her face in the light breeze until it was dry. She plaited it into one thick braid and flung it over her shoulder.

"I've been told there are wolves in these woods," said Thomas, coming to sit beside her where she'd started a small cook fire. He glanced at her, wondering how much she knew about wolves, not wanting to seem like a big brother. With so many sheep around Ramsay, wolves there seldom bothered humans. Elenor was smaller than most sheep.

"Wolves hate fire," he said, grasping a stick, one end of which was in the red center of the fire. He pulled it out and waved it, making orange loops in the night air. "This would slow them."

He'd skinned the rabbit and was roasting it over the fire. Elenor sat feeding in twigs absentmindedly, laziness creeping over her.

"Where's Etienne?" she asked Thomas.

"I think he'll stay away until we've eaten."

"Shall I go look for him?"

"No. He might be embarrassed."

"We'll save him a little then, shall we?"

Thomas was deep in a pleasant dream. Happiness wrapped him like a cocoon, like lamb's wool. Then suddenly it was ripped from him by a shriek.

He woke on his feet, sick at heart and shaking, heard the scream again and knew it came from outside him. He ran toward it. Marthe stood by her shelter, her hands over her collarbones, her face desolate. She grabbed his arm, shaking it.

"A wolf took Pipeau! I dreamed it, and when I woke he was gone! *Aiee! Pipeau!*"

Thomas held her by the shoulders.

"Do you know which way?"

Marthe ran to a big bush and fell on her knees. Thomas could see that the grass was flattened down, as if something had been dragged across it. He grabbed a stick from Marthe's fire, held it over his head, and strained his eyes to follow the flattened grass or any other trail marking. Carefully he made his way into the forest.

"Pipeau!" he shouted. "Call, Pipeau. Sing, Pipeau!" He concentrated every bit of his being on catching any whiff of child or animal, any sound, any warm current in the air. Nothing.

"Pipeau! Pipeau! Sing!"

He stood stock-still, straining his ears in the darkness.

To his amazement, he heard a tiny, thin voice, not more than ten yards away, cry, "Oat!" Thomas turned so fast he bashed his head into a tree branch. He found Pipeau on the ground, cold and dazed, one leg twisted. He picked up the child, who seemed weightless, but who clung to him like a barnacle. Thomas stood a minute in the dark, rocking the child, feeling through his own chest for a heartbeat, a pulse.

"Pipeau! Are you there?" At last he heard a tiny intake of breath, like a hiccup.

"Don't be afraid, Pipeau." He called out low and gently, "Marthe, come here. He lives."

He met her in the dark and gave Pipeau over to her. Marthe crooned and rocked as he had done.

Thomas came back through the dark, his face covered with blood.

Elenor had run to help but suddenly found herself shaking. "Bloody scalp wound," Thomas said, using a wet sock to clean up. "I hit a tree."

Elenor sat down, wrapped tight in her cloak, watching. *I should help,* she thought. *If I were a wife, I would help.* But she couldn't make herself move toward him or touch him. Thomas' large, pale face glowed ugly as a monster in the dimness. The blood running down beside his eye looked black.

As they cleaned camp next morning, Elenor noticed that Marthe was carrying Pipeau in a sling on her back as if he were a baby, while Guillemette, who was as slight as her brother, struggled to carry the baby on her hip. She went to find Thomas. The ugliness and kindness, so strong in him last night that she'd been afraid, were hidden in daylight like a secret.

"May I ask Marthe's children to ride with us?"

"We'll have to travel slowly."

Elenor nodded. "It's only as far as Bordeaux."

"All right," said Thomas, guessing that she had no idea how far away Bordeaux was. She went to talk to Marthe.

13

Book

From a baker drenched with sweat and powdered with flour, Thomas bought one loaf shaped like a crown, which he set on Guillemette's head, and a thin baguette that he presented to Pipeau as a sword.

"You ride," he told them. He walked down the road arguing with Etienne, holding Daisy's halter as she got used to carrying the two children.

A square tower dominated the road through Etampes. From tiny arrow slits it seemed to spy on passersby.

"Who lives there?" Elenor wondered, squinting up at them.

"A witch," Pipeau answered, pointing his sword and narrowing his eyes like Elenor.

"Long ago, almost a hundred years ago, the king of France locked his wife up in there," said Thomas, who was walking beside Elenor's stirrup.

He put a hand around her ankle. It circled completely, a protective cuff or a fetter.

"Why?" asked Guillemette.

"Because she was a witch, silly," said Pipeau. "Ask Thomas."

Elenor kicked loose and rode ahead.

"I never . . ." Thomas shook his head, and Pipeau laughed.

At a branching of the road outside Etampes they found a stone cross and a water trough for horses. One road led due south to Orléans, the other west to Chartres.

"Santiago is that way." Thomas pointed halfway between the two roads. "The southern road would get us to Bordeaux sooner." He spoke to Marthe, who was sitting on the grass nursing the baby.

"Thomas . . ." Etienne looked up from where he sat trying to pry a pebble from his sandal. "Chartres is the most beautiful of all cathedrals. Not only that, but—" His eyes shone. "There are book copiers! And in two days is the Feast of the Visitation. What better place to celebrate it?" He clasped his hands in an imploring gesture borrowed from a statue.

They all looked at each other, then at Thomas.

"Let's have Guillemette decide," said Elenor. "Will you, Guillemette? Look, I'll tie my sash

around your eyes, and spin you around, and whichever way you point, we'll go."

"Use my sword, Guillemette," said Pipeau.

"Yes," said Thomas. "That's the proper way to
do it."

"Will you *all* come with me wherever I go?"

"Yes, yes," they each assured her.

Elenor tied the sash around Guillemette's head
and took her to the middle of the road; she spun
the child by the shoulders and stepped back, leaving
her with her bare feet feeling out the dusty road,
clutching her skirt in one hand, the thin loaf of
bread held in the other like a wand.

"Turn, turn, turn, Guillemette," they sang and
clapped, and then, "That way!" she cried. She chose
the road to Chartres.

A wavery blob appeared on the road ahead of
them, about the size of a wide person, reddish
brown, moving in hops and jerks. On Daisy's back
the two children leaned forward, staring, mouths
open.

"How big do fleas get in these parts?" asked
Elenor.

"Big," said Etienne.

"Fattened on pilgrims," Thomas added.

Guillemette looked nervously from one to the

other. They neared the hopping form and made it out to be a man in a sack, holding the edge up close under his chin with both hands, his short gray beard poking over the top. He stopped, breathing heavily. Elenor glanced down and noticed that, except for the sack, he was naked.

"Greetings, brother," Elenor said politely.

"Greetings, sister, sir, ma'am," replied the man in the sack, bobbing his head toward each in turn.

"Are you going to Chartres?" asked Thomas.

"Aye, and in this bag, too," said the man.

"Why?" asked Pipeau, peering down at the man, speaking for them all. "Where are your small-clothes?"

"My boy," said the man with dignity, "where my smallclothes are is no concern of yours. My confessor has sent me on pilgrimage in this sack to take away my sin."

"Benedicite," said Thomas as they passed on by.

"Benedicite," they each murmured, and said no more until they were out of earshot. Guillemette was the first to speak.

"Nora, what's a confessor?"

"It's the priest who hears confessions."

"So the priest took his clothes?"

"Could happen," said Marthe calmly.

"And what is a visitation? Is there a story, Nora?"

"Yes."

Guillemette leaned back against Elenor, comfortable on Mab's broad back. "Tell it," she said.

"A long time ago," Elenor began, "there was a lady named Elizabeth, who was old and didn't have any children. So she prayed and prayed, and God decided to let her have a baby. God decided that her baby would be a great saint."

"Who?"

"Who did Elizabeth's baby grow up to be?"

"Yes, who?"

"Saint John the Baptist. He is the man who baptized Jesus and helped him preach."

Guillemette squirmed back hard against Elenor. "Tell me some more about when he was a baby."

"Well ... before John was born, the Angel Gabriel appeared to his father, whose name was Zacharias, while Zacharias was putting incense on the fire at the temple. The flames of the fire leaped up. The Angel Gabriel spoke like a trumpet: 'Zacharias, you are going to be a father!' Old Zacharias didn't believe him. He said, 'There must be some mistake.' So the angel said, 'You are going to be a father, and your son will be named John, and he will be great in the sight of the Lord.' Zacharias stood dumbfounded, with his mouth hanging open, just like you. So the Angel Gabriel added, 'Until the moment he is named, you will not be able to speak.' When Zacharias tried to ask the angel some questions, his mouth opened and closed, but he couldn't say a word.

"When Elizabeth was waiting for her baby to be born, her cousin came to visit her. And do you know who her cousin was?"

"A witch?" asked Guillemette.

"No! Think of the best lady that ever lived in the whole world."

"The Blessed Mother Mary!" shouted Guillemette.

"That's right!" Elenor said. "And the Blessed Mother Mary was Elizabeth's own cousin. That's who came to visit her, and that is why it is called the Visitation."

"She was lucky," Guillemette said enviously.

Along the road new wheat, combed and tossed by the breeze, turned in ribbons, green, gray, white. In the distance Chartres Cathedral rode like a ship, alone on the rolling waves of wheat, under a gray, windy sky.

"Oh!" Elenor stood up in her stirrups, leaning forward, the damp wind in her face, tears springing to her eyes. The cathedral was like a patch, joining earth and sky, part of both.

"It pulls heaven and earth together," she said. "How did they do it?"

"Skill and pride," said Thomas. "Probably sold their souls to the devil."

"Is knowledge the forbidden fruit, Thomas?" Etienne turned to walk backward, facing Thomas, his robe flapping in the wind.

"Only a small and jealous god would deny people the freedom to try to do beautiful things." Having the wind snatch away his words made Thomas feel free to say them.

"Or a small-minded church hierarchy, jealous of their power over people?" said Etienne, still walking backward, looking up at Thomas with raised eyebrows. The way he moved his hands made Elenor feel he was pulling away Thomas' doubts from him, taking away the mask of sarcasm.

"The story of Adam and Eve . . ." Thomas hesitated, and Elenor turned to listen. Thomas made a face as if he had bitten into a quince.

"I wonder," said Etienne, "how much *that* story has been bent."

"What . . . ?" began Elenor.

"Used for control, I mean, instead of for understanding. I hear it and can't find its truth anymore."

Elenor shivered. If stories could be bent . . . Suddenly she stood up in her stirrups. The scene at the play in Peterborough came back to her—Eve, with her hand outstretched, tempting Adam.

"It wasn't Eve's fault!" Elenor burst out. Etienne and Thomas stared at her.

"No," said Etienne slowly. "If Man is as fully human, as responsible as Woman, how could it have been?"

Thomas was watching Elenor and saw that she was pale and near tears. "But it's the Bible," she whispered.

"Don't be afraid, Nora!" said Etienne calmly. "It's human to wonder."

They traveled along in silence, and then Etienne spoke again.

"There is new wisdom sweeping the world. The University of Chartres had a teacher named Bernard—"

"Like me!" said Pipeau, waking up.

"Yes. This Bernard was a devout man, humble, and a wise theologian. As you may be, Pipeau. He taught that mankind is part of nature, created by God to help him create the world. Bernard wrote that the division between mankind and nature is a false one, because mankind is a part of nature, with particular, necessary intelligence and skill. Bernard said that to refuse to use that skill, whether out of humility or laziness, is to refuse God's intent."

Thomas thought this over. "Bernard believed that creation is still going on?" he asked.

"Yes," said Etienne.

"And that it would be sinful not to take part in it?"

"Yes!"

They rode for a while in silence, slowly, keeping pace with Etienne and with Marthe, who was on foot as always, carrying the baby.

"When I was seven," said Elenor, thinking aloud, "I planted my first garden. I planted peas. Father Gregory showed me how to make brush fences for them to climb on. I pulled out all the weeds, I watched for the peas every day, and I guarded them from bugs and rabbits. The leaves uncurled; the tendrils of vine came out and grabbed onto the brush; the vines grew up and flowered. Then slowly the pods formed behind the flowers and inside the pods little peas took shape. I could hold the pods up to the light and see the peas. I was so proud I couldn't sleep, and when I slept I dreamed of peas. And then I remembered: pride is sinful. I was ashamed to be happy. I went to confession to say that I had sinned."

"What did the priest say?" Etienne asked.

Elenor grinned, chin high. "He told me that I was helping God's creation. He said even God was proud on the sixth day. 'He saw that it was good.'"

Thomas thought of Father Gregory's stubby hands delicately tying back vines.

"Will they have a place for us to stay?" Marthe broke in. "Will there be a hostelry in Chartres?"

* * *

They passed together under the portico bright with painted statues. They passed through tall leather-covered doors. A draft of cold air met them, and the smell of human bodies and of incense and smoke. They stepped into a magical place of stone arches higher than any forest, and light of every color, rich beautiful colors exploding in starbursts and flowers. Pipeau clapped his hands and jumped around with his feet together, squealing in delight. Guillemette stood stock-still, her hands clasped and her mouth open. Marthe, holding the baby, fell on her knees on the stone floor.

They were told they could sleep in the cathedral. When the light faded from the windows, constellations of candles flared, stuck on iron spikes as thick as thorns on a thornbush, lighting up a compassionate Mother and Child here, a stern Saint Peter there, and in one corner Saint Nicholas, patron of students.

A deacon pulled a squeaking wagon across the stone floor. He threw out straw with a pitchfork, and pilgrims and poor gathered it into heaps to sleep on. Thomas went for water and to find where they could stable horses for the night. When he got back to the cathedral, he found the others all asleep.

Elenor had pillowed her head on Marthe's skirt; Guillemette had hers in the crook of Elenor's arm.

Thomas sat leaning against a pillar, looking at the downy curve of Guillemette's cheek, the thin nape of Pipeau's neck, the fine arch of Elenor's eyebrow. Then he stretched out flat on his back, content, with his head on his cloak. He slept soundly and woke only once, to the sound of monks chanting matins; the sound rose and spiraled like incense smoke up into the darkness at the top of the arches.

A deacon roused all the pilgrims before prime. Almost before they were on their feet, young oblates came by, sweeping the straw into piles, sloshing water over the floor where they had slept. Pipeau and Guillemette tried to follow the maze worked into the floor of the nave in colored stone. Elenor followed them, dizzy before they were half-way to the center of it.

Thomas stood while the Visitation mass was sung, dappled with color as the rising sun lit the rose window of the east. He rocked on his heels, humming.

Incense, singing, some long stretches of Latin. What Thomas wanted to do was to find somebody he could ask about hunting laws. He'd been warned near Beauvais that a man could get his nose cut off for snaring a rabbit, or hanged for shooting a deer. The warnings made him want to risk it. No, not now. He was responsible for the others. . . . Still, south of Chartres they would be going through game forest. Castle country, too. Castles meant different lords, each with his own way of enforcing the laws. As the Latin droned on, Thomas daydreamed a bonfire big enough to roast a deer, a deer fat enough to feed their whole group and over.

Elenor's mind floated in the music, on the play of light, and suddenly presented her with an idea: she would get a book for Thomas of the teachings of Bernard, the one Etienne had talked about. If only she could talk with Etienne alone, he might know where she could ask. She had never purchased anything so precious as a book, and the notion made her head spin.

"Ite! Missa est," the celebrant priest intoned.

"Deo gratias!" the crowd roared. Mass was over.

When Thomas took Marthe and the children to look at the saints in the portico, Elenor lagged behind and told Etienne her plan.

"Thomas!" he called. "Nora and I are off to get the horses!" They slipped away down a side street, running and skipping like truants once they were out of sight.

The area around the cathedral was full of copy shops, and it was not hard to find them, as each had windows and doors opened wide to let in light.

Clerks sat at tables, inkpots and quills at hand, originals propped carefully on pulpits such as Elenor had seen choristers use. Elenor and Etienne watched through a window as a copier carefully selected a squared-off sheet of parchment and, using a ruler and a pointed charred stick, made fine straight lines on it as a guide to where the letters should go. Then, at the beginning of the page, he drew a box. *That will be for the first letter,* thought Elenor. He left the box empty, looked carefully at his original, dipped his quill, tried a few experimental strokes on a dirtied parchment end, retrimmed the quill, and, finally satisfied, began his line of text.

The workshop was very quiet. Etienne signaled mutely to the proprietor and waited until the man came out into the street before greeting him warmly in dumb show. The bookseller had a handsome face with intent eyes, and lines of concentration drawing down the corners of his mouth. His shoulders were stooped. When he clasped Etienne by the elbows and smiled, all the lines of his face reversed themselves.

"Nora," Etienne said quietly, "this is a fellow student, Aimery. If anyone can tell us where to find a copy of the teachings of Bernard at pilgrim prices, it is he. Aimery is a man to whom books are like little sheep. He knows where they stray."

Aimery smiled, one hand still on Etienne's arm. "I have taken several copies in trade. The cheapest would be one in which the decorative squares have never been painted. Would you mind that?"

Elenor liked the idea very much. The book Aimery brought out was pleasingly plain and worn. Elenor could paint in the initial letters of each chapter herself and decorate them with flowers, animals, and people she saw along the way, when she got back home to Ramsay.

For this little book she parted with the emergency gold that Maude had sewn, in tiny coins, in the hem of her cape.

She had not thought before she got the book that it might be awkward to give Thomas a present. She had always given presents—flowers to Father Gregory, pretty pebbles to Carla, apples to Mab. But once she had thanked the bookseller and Etienne for their help and had the little book in hand, worry struck. How does a lady give a gift to her betrothed? She shook herself. To Etienne's surprise, she took off running through the streets, found Thomas not far from where she had left him, and thrust the book into his hand. "Here, Thomas, we have got you a present. I hope you will like it."

Thomas sat on the edge of the fountain and looked through the book. He liked its small chunkiness, its shabby softness. He liked turning the pages and seeing the words marching along like knights with their lances up. He liked to think of the ideas that would be in such a book, ideas he could remind himself of as often as he wanted, once he had made himself remember how to read.

14

Frogs and Owls

The trees had grown lush and heavy in their greenness and hung over the road brushing the faces of the riders. Deer stood in the forest and watched them with gentle, wary eyes. Hunting was strictly forbidden. Marthe, Elenor, and the children gathered mushrooms in the woods, using their hats as baskets. Marthe showed Elenor which ones were good to eat and made her take off her heavy sandals and wiggle her toes in the soft, cool forest loam. Deep underneath the loam they found black truffles, which Marthe called the best of wild edibles.

The Order of Saint Benedict ran a rest house for pilgrims a day's walk south of Chartres. At table they heard stories of hunger to the south. Elenor and Guillemette contributed their mushrooms to the abbey kitchen and were rewarded with sweet cakes by the cook.

The next evening their path approached a clearing, and they heard a high droning that at first Thomas took for bees. As he was thinking how he might extract wild honey and what they would do with it, having no bread, and whether it would be worth the risk of stings, the droning resolved into children's voices singing. In the clearing rose a castle with cone-shaped turrets, flying the banners of a lord of the church. It was prettily reflected in a moat green with lily pads and weeds. Around the outside of the moat, children lined the bank, each holding a long pole and slapping the water in rhythm, chanting a song. They all turned their heads to watch the approaching pilgrims. The song wavered to a stop.

"Good evening, friends. What are you doing, and what song are you singing?" Elenor asked.

At first the children only giggled and murmured to one another. Then two of them pushed forward a third, a little girl with uncombed hair and a tattered dress, who, staring at her feet, said quickly, "Madame, we are beating the frogs, so that they will not croak tonight and wake our lord abbot." Then she looked up and gave Elenor a brief, lovely smile.

"Are you singing to the frogs?" asked Elenor, her head tilted to one side.

"Yes. So that they will know why we are bonking them." Some of the other children laughed again.

"May we listen while you work?"

Without answer the little girl ran back and seized her pole, calling to the others, "Come on, we must bonk the frogs. Sing!"

> *"Peace, frog, don't peep.*
> *Here comes the abbot*
> *Whom God keep."*

"Do they hurt the frogs?" Guillemette asked anxiously.

"I think the frogs are smart and stay underwater, where they won't get hurt," Elenor said.

Thomas thought differently. He didn't say anything, but he called a halt farther along the path, and while the others gathered firewood, he took his hat and ran back to the castle moat. On his way he picked up a branch to use as a rake. When he got to the moat, he found some of the children preparing to go home. To a boy who was looking at him suspiciously, he explained, "I am worried that some of these dead frogs will smell bad for Monsieur l'Abbé, so I am going to throw them into the forest."

So saying, he carefully raked in a few dozen stunned frogs, put them in his hat, threw the branch into the woods, and waved to the children. The boy who had been watching him nodded sagely.

"My father does that, too," he remarked.

Thomas was pleased. He soon had a small cook fire going, and a savory dish of frogs' legs, truffles, and wild garlic. It was the next best thing to hunting.

Toward evening they reached a tiny church in the forest. Over the door was a carving of Saint George on horseback slaying a dragon.

"Look, Pipeau!" said Guillemette. "A man on a horse killing a flea."

"Welcome," said the priest of the church. "We have pallets in the cloister for pilgrims. You are welcome to sleep there."

Thomas, Elenor, and Etienne looked at one another.

"Thank you, Father." Thomas spoke for them. "If we may fill our gourds at your well, we would like to camp nearby." The priest lifted his hand in blessing.

Marthe and her children stayed in the cloister. "I want good stone walls around me, thank you," she said, holding the children close. And to Elenor she added in a whisper, "The cook says there are ghosts in those woods. Be careful, now, and stay near the others."

Etienne and Elenor dragged fallen branches into a pile, while Thomas nursed a tinder spark to flame, feeding it dry leaves and wood shavings, blowing on it gently. As they sat down to rest, Etienne dropped something into Elenor's hand. "For the book," he said. It was a tiny tree snail, its shell delicately striped. Elenor held it in her palm, looking at it this way and that, memorizing its lines, hoping that some chapter of Thomas' book began with *O*.

The fire flared suddenly.

"That should discourage wolves," said Thomas.

And ghosts, Elenor thought. "I wonder why ... What sort of ghosts was Marthe talking about?"

"Best not think about it," said Etienne, but Thomas stretched with a gleam in his eye.

"A ghost like the Maiden of Peterborough," he said.

"Who is she?" Elenor moved closer to the fire, closer to her companions.

Thomas gave her a stern look under his black eyebrows. "You don't know about the Maiden of Peterborough?"

Elenor shook her head.

"You're too young."

Elenor scowled.

"Tell us, tell us," said Etienne in imitation of Guillemette, looking from one to the other.

Thomas stared solemnly into the fire.

"The story was told to me by a young man I met at the fair in Peterborough. A sad-looking young man, a student perhaps, too tied to his books to enjoy life. He told me that only a year ago, on All Hallows' Eve, he had been riding from Thornham to Peterborough along the open road. It was a dark and stormy night. Much to his surprise he saw a girl standing alone by the side of the road. Her cape was pulled tight around her, but her face was so beautiful it seemed to shine in the gloom. Thinking that she must be in some distress, he reined in his horse. 'What might I do to help you?' he asked. The girl, whose lovely pale face he could barely make out, said that she had been traveling to her father's house with the son of a lord with whom she was in service. The lordling had made advances. She had resisted, so angering him that he had put her off his horse to walk alone on the road.

"The student was moved to pity. He feared for her, alone in the storm, so he invited her to ride behind him, saying, 'Let me deliver you to your father's doorstep.' She mounted behind him, put her hands around his waist, and off they rode together. The student could feel her warm breath on his neck. He turned his mind to psalms, to Bible verses, to the sermons of Bishop Jerome.... At length he saw a light in the distance, a rush torch burning smokily in the doorway of a peasant hovel. He turned on his horse, asking the girl, 'Is this your father's house?' He found himself talking to the air. He turned around and around on the road. Could the girl have fallen asleep and slipped off the horse? There was no one on the road as far as he could see. Baffled, he dismounted and knocked at the door of the hovel. Finally it was opened a crack by a rheumy-eyed old man. 'Ah! Botherin' me agin, are ye! Well, begone! Aye, she was my daughter, but she's dead now these past ten years. It's only once a year, on All Hallows' Eve, the night she died, that she stops somebody on the road to ask for a ride home.' "

A silence fell, broken only by the croaking of frogs. The fire crackled. Elenor's arms were bumpy with gooseflesh.

"And now," said Etienne, "let me tell you about the man with the leg of gold. . . ."

In the middle of the night, Elenor woke to the deep eerie call of an owl. Fright seized her, and the longer she lay quietly, the more scared she felt. She thought of the girl on the road and wanted to cry. She thought that if she turned, she might see the maiden, standing pale and sorrowful, just behind her.

Thomas' back loomed next to her like a rock. She shook him until he turned over sleepily. The fire was out, and she couldn't see his face.

"There's an owl." How could she explain without sounding like a baby?

After a moment, Thomas put an arm around her, and rolled her over so that her back was against him. "It's good to know there's an owl close by," he said thoughtfully, "because owls, as you know, are guardians against ghosts and demons. Ghosts never come anywhere near where an owl has been."

Elenor knew no such thing, but she pretended he was Carla, who knew everything, snuggled against him, and slept.

15

The Lady
in the Barrow

Her hair was wild as dandelion fluff, but whiter. Her eyes were round and black as a bird's. They met her on the road to Vendôme, perched in a wheelbarrow. She sat proudly on a cushion, clutching the sides of the barrow, while a hefty, cheerful man held the handles and pushed a zigzag course between ruts and holes.

"What a pretty baby you have there, daughter!" the old lady called to Marthe.

"I hope he will grow up to be as strong as your son," replied Marthe.

"Where are you traveling to?" asked Thomas.

"He works in Vendôme," said the old lady, tossing her head back toward the man, "on the cathedral."

"I'm a glassblower," he said. "Been living in a lodge with the other journeymen, but now my ma's coming to live with me, I've got a cottage."

"How is the work?" Thomas wanted to know.

"Eh?" The glassblower sucked in his cheeks and poked out his lips. The effect was so intriguing that Elenor tried it, too, and felt like a fish. "Vendôme's a good place for the things that make up glass. Beech trees grow along the river. We burn the trees for heat, and use the ash to mix with sand for the glass."

"Hotter than hell, those ovens," put in his mother, with a nod of satisfaction.

The man was sweating.

"We have water," Elenor said. "Would you like some?"

They halted in the shade of a tree. The man lifted his mother from the barrow as easily as one might pick up a bird from its nest, and set her on her feet, puffing out his cheeks as he did so, like a lizard. Marthe took the old lady's arm and helped her walk up and down, getting her legs working after the ride. Sitting on a bank, they passed Elenor's gourd from hand to hand, pouring cool spring water mixed with wine down their dusty throats. The man scooped up a handful of sand from the side of the road. White and fine, it powdered through his fingers and sparkled in the sun.

"Look at it," he said. "And the sand from the river bottom is better yet. I'm Jacques, and my mother here is Sybille."

"But you may call me Nana," Sybille said.

"Thank you," said Elenor. Now she had two nanas.

"What part of the work do you do?"

"I keep the ovens going. Sometimes I blow. Sometimes I spin."

"Spin what?"

"Spin out the plates."

"What's that?" asked Thomas.

"Patience," said Jacques.

The cottage Jacques had rented perched on the riverbank, one room, square and solid.

"Stay, stay! All of you!" Nana Sybille insisted.

Etienne gathered a fistful of weeds and bunched them together into a broom. He swept out the fireplace first, carefully setting aside bits of charcoal he knew Elenor would want for drawing. Everything else—ashes, birds' nests, spiderwebs—he swept out the door. Then he laid a careful fire.

Elenor went to haul drinking water from the town fountain while Thomas watered the horses in the river. Marthe made a pallet for Pipeau in one corner. Thomas gave Elenor coins to go marketing for supper, and Sybille lent her the wheelbarrow. She trundled Guillemette down the road toward the market, wobbling, laughing, shouting. Thomas could hear Guillemette's persistent voice: "Can we get carrots, Nora? Can we get strawberries?"

Thomas was dumbfounded by his companions' burst of domesticity in such a small space. Escaping the broom, the wash water, the search for a cooking pot, he almost stepped on Pipeau. He went walking outside, feeling useless. He pulled a few weeds around Sybille's house. His father's voice echoed unwanted in his ears. "The duty of a noble is to protect the people and administer justice." Ha! He would give much for a staunch and useful duty, such as cooking, or cutting stone, or transforming sand to glass. . . .

"Now!" said Jacques, coming up behind Thomas. Empty-hearted, glad of distraction, Thomas followed him over to the glassmakers' yard.

Though it was late afternoon, people were still at work. Two of the large white ovens were smoking.

"Just watch," said Jacques. He picked up the bellows and puffed air on the already red coals, causing them to burst into flame. He checked a liquid mixture that was bubbling inside the stove. He took a long pipe that was leaning against the oven and put one end of it in the mixture, turning it round and round until the molten glass stuck on the pipe in a thick knob. Then he pulled the pipe out of the oven, held it straight ahead of him like a trumpet, and continuing all the while to twirl it, blew on the end of the pipe. The glass at the other end began to swell. When the glass balloon was as big as a man's head, Jacques stopped blowing, but kept twirling the pipe, keeping the balloon of even size. At a nod from Jacques, a bystander took a caliper and quickly cut off the end of the balloon. Jacques twirled harder. The balloon flattened out into a round disk of glass, two fingers thick and as big around as a barrow wheel. Jacques continued to twirl it, more and more slowly as it hardened, the muscles on his arms standing out, bulging, working, shifting. At last the glass became completely solid. Jacques carried it to a bench, and gently cracked it free of the pipe.

"Plate," said Jacques, tapping the disk.

Carrying the new plate, Jacques led Thomas inside the workshop. On the tops of benches coated with thick white plaster, designs for parts of the cathedral windows were drawn in bold black lines. At one bench, a man had laid a disk of red glass over the design and cut the glass to fit a piece of the picture, the top of a man's robe. At another table a man was fitting together several pieces of glass with strips of lead. Thomas could see the arms and hands and beard of the figure; there was a space ready for the piece of red robe.

Jacques gave Thomas some pebble-sized drops of colored glass. Thomas slipped them in his pouch to give to Guillemette and Pipeau. Or maybe to make a necklace for the Brat, someday.

Thomas and Jacques found supper ready at the cottage, flowers on the windowsill, and stew bubbling.

Around the fire after supper, tired as they were, no one wanted to go to sleep. Elenor sat on the floor next to Nana Sybille and tried not to stare at Jacques' arms. She had tried to draw them earlier, to catch in charcoal the way the veins ran over muscle like water over stone, and had failed utterly.

"Tell us a story, Nora," said Guillemette.

Elenor shook her head. "My mind is fished out of stories."

There was a silence.

"Ma knows a ton of stories," said Jacques. Nana Sybille watched them all with shiny black eyes. She threw back her head and laughed her high squeaky laugh. Her little face was flushed by the warmth of the fire; her hair glowed pink.

"I could tell you the story of the proud knight and the Loathsome Lady," she said, and suddenly reached down, patted Elenor's knee, and added in a whisper, "Do you think *I'm* a loathsome lady, just because I'm old?"

"You are a lovely, lovely lady," whispered Elenor. Sybille folded her hands and began her story, her voice now different, dreamy and slow.

"Once, in the old times of elves and fairies, there lived a most unpleasant knight, proud and lusty, with no courtesy. One day as he was riding through the woods, he met a young maid all alone, and by force he carried her off to his castle. She was no fool, and she found means to escape from him, and when she had escaped, she went to the king to ask that her honor be avenged, that the knight be punished. When the king inquired into the matter, he found that the maid was virtuous and true to her word, and that the knight had done such wicked deeds before. It was determined that he should lose his life in punishment. All the court was gathered together when the knight came to receive his sentence. He strode among them so bravely and cut such a handsome figure that the queen could not bear to think of him being beheaded, so she begged the king, 'Since the wrong was done to a woman, will you not let a woman decide on the sentence?' The king decided that this would be just. The queen then called out to the knight and said, 'Sir Knight, you have done a wicked thing, and it is right that you should die for it. But because we women are merciful, I will give you one chance to save your life. If within one year you can find the answer to my question, an answer that no woman shall argue with, then you shall have your life and freedom.'

" 'I thank my lady,' said the knight, making a deep bow. 'What is the question?'

" 'You must find out what it is that women want the most,' said the queen.

"Now the knight had never thought about this question. He had no idea what the answer would be. He galloped all over the kingdom asking everyone the question and he did not find a single village, a single town, where two people could agree on the answer. On the very last evening before he had to go back to the queen, he was riding through a forest and heard strange and beautiful music. At first it seemed to come from the air, but he looked up and saw nothing unusual. Then it seemed to come from the ground, so he got off his horse to listen more closely. On the ground he thought he saw a ring of fairies dancing, but when he bent to peer more closely, they disappeared. Dizzy and befuddled, he looked up, and there before him he saw the most loathsome old woman he had ever seen, crouched like a toad beside a large tree.

" 'Greetings, Sir Knight,' she croaked.

"Without even returning her salutation, the knight jumped on his horse, ready to ride away from there as quickly as possible.

" 'I know the answer to your question,' croaked the old woman.

"The knight reined in his horse.

" 'If you could tell me the answer to my question,' said the knight, 'I would be greatly in your debt.'

" 'Yes, you would,' agreed the crone. 'You would owe me your very life. And if I told you the answer, and if my answer were accepted by the queen and all her ladies, would you promise to do for me anything that lies within your power to do?'

"Without hesitation the knight said, 'Certainly, my lady.'

" 'Then put your head down close and I will whisper the answer in your ear.'

"Reluctantly, the knight got off his horse and put his ear close to the old woman's mouth, and she whispered to him.

"The knight rode hard all the next day and came in the evening to the hall of the king and queen. The queen had gathered all her ladies: the noble matrons, the heady young girls, the widows who have the grace of wisdom. Peasant women came as well, and all the scrubbing girls and cooks. Among these was one old and very ugly crone, the woman of the forest.

"The queen gave orders that the knight should tell them all what it was that women wanted most.

"The knight's answer rang out in the hall: 'My liege and lady,' he said, 'a woman wants sovereignty: she wishes to direct her own will.'

"There was a murmur in the hall, and the queen asked the ladies of the court, 'Shall he live?'

"The ladies all answered, 'Yes, he should live, for he has spoken well.'

"Then, before the celebrations could begin, the old woman of the forest spoke up: 'Your mercy, sovereign lady queen! Before the court disperses, do me right! I am the one who gave the knight the answer he has given you, and he has pledged to do for me whatever lies within his power to do. Before you all, I ask that he take me for his wife.' A hush fell on the company.

" 'Old lady, for God's love, think of a new request!' begged the knight. 'Take all my goods, but leave my body free.'

" 'No,' said the crone. 'I may be foul, I may be poor and old, yet for all the gold in the world, I would not be other than your wife, nay, than your very love.'

" 'My love,' muttered the knight rudely. 'My damnation, more likely.'

"But the assembly of ladies insisted that he keep his word, so in sad and solemn ceremony he and the old crone were wed. He took his ancient wife upon his arm, and they retired to their chamber, where he hid like an owl. That night, the knight lay on his side of the bed tossing and turning. His ancient wife lay smiling by his side. At length she said, 'Bless us! Is this how knights and wives get on together here? Are all the knights here so contemptuous? Tell me, how may I put things to rights?'

" 'Put things to rights!' groaned the knight. 'Nothing can ever be right for me again.'

" 'And why not?' asked his wife.

" 'Because you are old and ugly, poor and low-bred, that's why.'

" 'I am old, and you gentlemen do pledge yourselves to honor age.

" 'I am ugly, and having an ugly wife, you may rest free of the envy and desires of others.

" 'As for my poverty, which you reprove, Almighty God himself did choose a life of poverty. The truly poor are they who whine and fret, coveting what they cannot hope to get. To others poverty is an incentive to livelihood, and a help in our capacity for wisdom.

" 'You speak of low birth, and reproach me for it, but gentleness is not inherited along with the title of earl or knight. You'll often find some lordling full of villainy and shame. Vice and bad manners are what make a churl, not lowly birth. To him who intends to do what deeds of gentleness he can, God gives gentility. That we are gentle comes to us by grace.'

"The knight lay still, his arm covering his eyes.

" 'Given the choice,' continued his wife, in a tone that was both stern and gentle, 'would you have me old and ugly till I die, but still a loyal, wise, and humble wife, or would you rather I be young and pretty, not yet wise, and take your chances with those who come to see you on account of me. Which would you have? The choice is yours.'

"The knight pondered all she had said. At last he spoke: 'My lady and my wife, I leave the matter to your wise decision. Do what you think best, and what will best do honor to us both. Whatever pleases you suffices me.'

" 'Then you have recognized my sovereignty,' said she.

" 'Aye,' said the knight, and took his arm away from his eyes.

" 'And you have chosen well,' said she, 'for you will find me now both fair and faithful as a wife.'

"The knight looked at his wife and saw that she was both lovely and wise, and as he himself was wiser than he had been, they lived together long and happily."

* * *

There was a comfortable silence around the fire. Pipeau snored and shifted in his sleep. Elenor, who sat on the floor next to Nana Sybille's chair, took the old lady's hand and held it against her cheek.

"That was a good story," she said.

"The knight got off too easy," said Marthe. "The women should have just ..." She drew a finger across her neck.

"Do you think all women want the same thing?" asked Thomas.

Elenor saw that he was asking her.

"I think that most want sovereignty over their own lives, but that only some want to rule their husbands' lives as well."

A smile touched Thomas' face. He looked back into the fire.

16

Mulberries

T homas leaned his elbows on a table outside a tavern, under the canopy of a mulberry tree. Guillemette had made herself a collar of the broad green mulberry leaves, and Pipeau was collecting purple berries to eat. Chickens pecked around their feet, their necks and breasts stained purple, waddling fatly. On a shard that she'd found by the wayside, Elenor sketched in charcoal Guillemette's round face, her thin neck, and the collar of leaves. Etienne watched over her shoulder, keeping his distance.

"These are fine big trees," Thomas remarked to the tavern keeper. "I've never seen such trees anywhere."

The tavern keeper's wife began proudly, "Oh, but they're mulberries—"

"Shut up, fool," whispered the tavern keeper. "Foreign spies."

"Are the berries good for your poultry?" Thomas

asked the wife, pretending not to have heard. Touraine had been an English fief until barely fifty years ago, and the English were hated. "Your chickens look very stout."

The tavern keeper grunted, and offered wine around. Etienne was out of stories; the children were cranky. Marthe sat wordlessly drinking her wine. At any moment, Thomas thought, she would topple over, snoring on the table. Rain fell steadily but had not yet made its way through the thick foliage above them.

"Is there a place we pilgrims could roll out our cloaks and sleep?" Thomas asked. The tavern keeper jerked his head at his wife, who followed him inside their door. They conferred in whispers.

"Don't trust the ape-man," came the taverner's voice. "He talks like an Englishman and a lord at that. He asks too many questions and his eyes are everywhere."

Outside, Thomas leaned his jaw on his hand, listening hard. Elenor smiled to herself. Ape-man?

"The children are very tired, and the others, too. What harm can it do to let them sleep here?" the wife asked.

There was a tearing sound as the taverner scratched his chin.

"Let them sleep in the house," his wife begged

in her soft, whispery voice. "They won't hurt your precious worms!"

"The guild chief says it's a secret, right? You know what a secret is, woman?"

Thomas wiggled his eyebrows at Elenor. She tiptoed to the door to hear better.

". . . then I can keep an eye on them, and perhaps they will pay us a little something, too. Wheat is so dear these days it's been a week since—"

"Woman!"

Elenor jumped backward.

"All right, woman, I'll let you have your way this once. But you be the one to stay awake and keep watch over them."

Elenor scurried back to the table as the taverner and his wife emerged with foxy smiles to invite them inside.

Early in the morning, Thomas went out and stumbled on an elevated pen full of mulberry leaves, swarming with life. He wondered if his eyes were playing tricks on him, and bent closer. Worms! Worms were crawling all over the leaves, devouring them, leaving only the laciest of leaf skeletons. Thomas watched in fascinated revulsion. Why, in time of famine, would someone be feeding worms? Did the taverner cook them and feed them to wayfarers? Thomas thought of last night's soup.

Wait—silk was spun from the filament of worms. Was the taverner making silk? If so, he must be working with other people. The taverner was not the sort to have developed such a scheme on his own. And a brilliant scheme it was, with ships vying to bring silks from the East at great expense.

Thomas turned to go up to the house, interested in his discovery, hoping the others would be ready to be on their way.

"Ha!"

"Halt!"

"Ho!"

Three men jumped in front of him, jabbing pitchforks at his chest. One was the taverner himself. Another was a broad man with a beard and small eyes. The third had the large frightened eyes of a deer, a slack jaw, and a forehead beaded with sweat.

"Spy!" spat the taverner. "What did I tell you? Come along with us now."

"Where do we take him, Henri?" asked the wide-eyed man. He prodded Thomas like a hog to be gotten to market.

"To the guild, I'd say."

"Aye. Take him before the guild."

"Or—"

Rage swept Thomas. He grabbed the nearest pitchfork by its middle tine, wrenched it from the taverner's grasp, and swung it in a wide arc. There was the joy of a blow well connected, as the pitch-fork cracked against the doe-eyed man's jaw and sent him flying.

Thomas flung down the pitchfork: he had lifted his hand against another, while under oath not to. The taverner and the bandy-legged man had scattered to a safe distance. When they saw the Englishman standing stock-still, they returned cautiously, and when they saw that he offered no resistance, they tied his hands.

"You have broken the code of the pilgrim, Englishman," said Henri gloatingly, once Thomas' hands were secured behind his back.

"You're not as dumb as I thought, Henri," Thomas said, in English. The third man stumbled to his feet, spit out a gob of blood, and eyed Thomas balefully. The three of them argued in harsh voices. Then they pushed Thomas up toward the house.

"Take him before the Knights Templar," said Henri's wife. "They are the ones responsible for the behavior of pilgrims. And they are rich; they should reward us for our trouble."

The other men nodded.

"Your woman's right. If we took him to the head of the guild, and he is a spy, then we'd be in trou—"

Henri cut him short. "Fix us some traveling food, then, woman. We'll take the pack of them to the Templars and see what satisfaction we can get."

At the first shouts, Pipeau and Guillemette had slipped into their clothes and gathered the baby's rags from the bushes where they were drying, and now they clung to Marthe's skirts.

Elenor stood alone. *Thomas will go to jail,* she thought. *I have no choice but to go with him.*

"Marthe." Elenor's eyes filled with tears. "Maybe we can catch up with you somewhere farther along."

Marthe looked around at all the others, bit her fingernail, rearranged Guillemette's hair. "No," she said. "It may take a little longer to get to Bordeaux, but we would rather stay with you." Pipeau and Guillemette nodded solemnly.

"And you, Etienne, you should—"

Etienne shook his head. "The Templars' headquarters are at Ozon, to the south. It's on our way, Nora! I've got to see what those Templars will do to my wild friend Thomas."

"I'll beat 'em up," said Pipeau.

The Knights Templar, self-appointed guardians of the Pilgrim Way, had built their headquarters in their own image. Harsh and gray and proud,

Ozon towered above the road. Elenor thought the king himself would feel like a supplicant approaching Ozon, and was surprised that Henri had the nerve to take them there. She sat tall as she could stretch on Mab's back, with a lump in her throat. Suppose the Templars put them all in dungeons? She looked at her companions: they seemed like a ragged troupe of mummers, still in costume. Henri played the rogue, with his suspicious face, his shifty eyes, his ragged peasant clothes; Guillemette and Pipeau were child martyrs, their pinched faces appearing over clenched knuckles as they held on to the side of Henri's cart. Marthe sat on a pile of straw in one corner of the cart, nursing her baby, a Nativity scene from a Christmas pageant. Etienne sat with Antoine, the man whom Thomas had struck, their feet dangling over the back of the cart. Antoine's jaw was swollen and purple, his big eyes slightly crossed.

Thomas rode alongside the cart, reflecting fondly on the virtues of his horse, Daisy. She had kicked Henri when he tried to ride her, and left a steaming pile of manure right in front of his door. Even now she was prancing, arching her neck and lifting her hooves proudly.

Thomas' ribs were sore from the prodding of Henri's pitchfork. He tried to put himself in a

penitent frame of mind, but flexed his fingers, looking forward to the day he would no longer be a
pilgrim, under this cursed vow of nonviolence.

The master of the Ozon Knights Templar
looked down his long thin nose at Henri and
dismissed him with a pouch of coins disdainfully
thrown. When he called Thomas before him,
Etienne slipped in, too, and stood beside Thomas
as a witness. The master's voice was clipped and
precise, and as he spoke he surveyed Thomas with
pale blue eyes, sizing him up for usefulness as if he
were a sword or a saddle.

"Your breach of the code is a serious offense,
regardless of the provocation. The lands between
here and the Pyrenees are in a state of unrest. There
has been, as you have doubtless heard, a drought in
Poitou, and now there is famine. Pilgrims are not
welcome. Pilgrims who travel alone or in small
groups are particularly suspect. I have the authority
to impose certain sanctions on you, and I will do
so. I require that you join with the group of pilgrims
who are presently in Poitiers awaiting an escort,
and that you make yourself responsible for them in
every way. I require that you escort this group until
you have crossed the border of Navarre and have
seen them safely to the hospice of Sancti Spiritus,

seeing that none of this group breaks away to try to travel alone. You will confess here, and stay the night. There will be an early mass tomorrow morning.

No, thought Thomas. *Put me in stocks. Give me one hundred lashes. Don't put me in charge of a flock of religious fanatics.*

Without waiting for questions, the master turned on his heel and left.

In Poitiers Thomas put his companions to work. "Round up the pilgrims, men," he said, with as much enthusiasm as if he had been talking about hedgehogs or leeches. Elenor, Guillemette, and Pipeau stared at him.

"We'll go to the hospice," Marthe said. "Nora and I can talk to people there."

"I'll take the churches and streets north of here, and Etienne, you take the south side. We'll leave tomorrow morning, after mass, from in front of the church of the Benedictines."

"Yes, sir!" said Elenor. "Step sharply there, Captain Pipeau."

The Benedictine hostelry was crowded, stifling, and full of the sad cries of children. Pilgrims flopped on cots or leaned on walls, tired and restless, red-eyed from the dust of dry roads. Children lay with their faces flat on the stone floor, trying to cool off.

Etienne rounded up seven Flemish students who had joined the Way, and four German burghers, all members of the butchers' guild.

Thomas found six of the prisoners who had been released in Paris, still together, less pale and more rowdy after a month on the road.

Elenor found four nuns, a quarrelsome self-anointed saint, a trinket merchant, and a very old friar.

In all, more than fifty pilgrims banded together for the journey from Poitiers to the Pyrenees.

After mass the next morning they left the city, a motley, impatient group. Thomas rode up and down the Way, trying to count people and to notice faces, trying to know and to care if anyone needed help.

17

Poitou

It was spring in Poitou, but felt like late summer. Along the dry road, walkers and horses kicked up a thick worm of dust. Elenor walked, a shirt tied across her face, so that the children could ride high and breathe clearly. Thomas picked his way on Daisy, whose eyelashes were coated white with dust, riding at the back of the convoy, counting, carrying water for those who lagged.

On either side of the Way, new crops withered in the fields. There was no place to stop. From behind mud walls embedded with sticks, mean and hungry dogs strained at their chains and barked at the pilgrims, warning them away, and when Thomas braved the dogs to ask for water, he was met by peasants armed with pikes. Angry and polite, he bought water at exorbitant prices for everyone.

They blame us for the drought, Elenor thought.

Looking at the column of pilgrims plodding silently in front of her, it was easy to see them as insects, a plague of big, black, hungry ants. Doomsdayers. She shivered, hot in her body and cold in her soul.

They made one cool stop, in a wayside church where even the holy water had been lapped up by dog or pilgrim. No priest came out to bless them, but children lay on the floor or pressed their tired faces against stone columns, and many crawled into dark corners to sleep out of the sun. They prayed to survive, to get through, and they prayed for rain.

Marthe's baby, Jean-Paul, was shrinking. Under his sparse hair, the top of his head dipped in, and his eyes sank deeper. Elenor thought he looked ancient, saw he might die, and, dizzy with thirst, pretended she wasn't. She gave her share of water to Marthe so that she would have milk in her breasts. Marthe said nothing, but trudged on determinedly.

"In four days," Thomas told her, "we should be in Bordeaux."

A day later an old friar called Pietro and a lame ex-prisoner lagged so much that stronger pilgrims took turns carrying them piggyback. To slow the pace of the column endangered everyone. Seeing a village in the distance, they all hoped against hope for bread, water, a swig of wine, a blessing in the church. As they drew near, they heard shutters slam shut on the houses. Though the Way passed through the center of town, few people were out, and these jeered and shouted at the pilgrims to keep them from stopping. As Elenor, Guillemette, and Pipeau, all three on Mab, passed a group of women, one turned and spat on them. Hungry and furious, Elenor rode up beside Thomas, maneuvering Mab with a kind of careless skill, glad for once to be above people.

"I hate them!" she said. "I asked nothing of her. I wouldn't eat her bread if she brought it to me on a platter."

"I would," said Thomas. He hadn't eaten anything in two days, and even the thought of bread made him ache. "It isn't us they hate. It's hunger."

Elenor shook off his hand. "Oh, *good,* sir," she said sarcastically. "Dogs snarl when they're hungry. These are supposed to be people." She kicked her heels hard into Mab's flanks.

Guillemette dug her head into Elenor's back. "Sir is Thomas?" she asked.

Thomas turned away, and Elenor reined in, feeling sad and mean. She was snarling herself, and her anger had not been against Mab or Thomas.

Shouts and dust rose up ahead of them.

"The well," Thomas said. They edged nearer the center of the fray. Pilgrims were flocking to refill their water gourds, with dust-coated faces and hands outstretched. Peasants with pikes and staves stood in a circle, their backs to the well, guarding their precious water.

Women peeked from behind shutters. Men and boys slipped from house doors, clubs or knives tucked under their arms. Elenor watched from Mab's back. The pilgrims who were still far from the well, on foot, could see nothing, and longed for water. They pressed forward. Elenor could hear the shuffle of their feet, and a low moan from the pilgrims close to the well and the pikes, who were trying to stop.

Elenor saw Thomas cup his hands into a trumpet to make his voice reach the armed peasants.

"People of Poitou," he said, "we come in peace, on pilgrimage, as you see. Do you have water that you can share with us?"

The men around the well stood solidly. Some shifted their pikes to form a fence. Thomas spoke again.

"Are you short of water here?"

"Aye, we're short of water!"

"And we're tired of pilgrims, too."

"We've had a bellyful of you pious leeches."

"Of that and nothing else!"

"What good will your prayers do us? We'll be starved before you reach Compostela."

The shouts grew into a shrill clamor. Thomas lifted his hand.

"What do we have that we can give you in return for water? What can we offer you besides . . . prayers?"

Elenor felt her heart shrink. She knew what they had.

A man holding a hatchet was the first to answer.

"You could give us your fine horse." His friends cheered him.

Thomas must have known what would be asked of him, for with a calm that astounded Elenor, he said, "My beautiful horse will stay with you, if you treat her gently and have need of her, and if you will give all of these pilgrims permission to drink and to fill their gourds at your well."

A sound like the wind came from the pilgrims, a whistle of incredulity. Never did a knight part willingly with his horse. His horse was rank, class, heritage.

"How can he leave Daisy with these mean, mean people?" Elenor asked Etienne, tears streaming down her face.

"They won't eat her," Etienne said. "She's too valuable."

Some of the pilgrims, too weak to walk farther that day, slept in the village church. Thomas longed to be alone. Too many were making a fuss over him. A woman had kissed his foot.

Thomas, Elenor, and Etienne camped outside the village, keeping their fire bright so that the other pilgrims would not feel abandoned. Elenor stroked Mab, combing and calming her. Close to the campfire, Etienne talked to Thomas. Elenor watched the firelight play on their faces, making deep shadows. Both looked gaunt. It was good to see Thomas laugh.

"Brat, come hear this. Etienne has memorized a guidebook for pilgrims, written by a priest from these parts. Listen to what he says about the people of Poitou."

Thomas had unrolled her cloak beside him. She lay down on her stomach, her hands under her chin, and watched Etienne strike a pompous pose, his hand over his heart.

"The Poitevins are vigorous people and good warriors, able in handling bows and arrows and war spears, brave in battle, very fast runners, elegant in their manner of dress"—Etienne hitched up his sleeves fastidiously—"beautiful of face, witty, generous, and . . . of great hospitality!"

Oh, Etienne, if you make me laugh, I'll surely cry, thought Elenor, but she put her head down and slept instead.

18

Heroes

We are the great dust caterpillar, Grendel the Worm with a hundred feet," Elenor told Guillemette.

Pipeau coughed and closed his eyes. He wobbled in front of Elenor, and she steadied him with her forearms, which felt stiff as sticks.

The pilgrim caravan pressed on toward the southwest, faster, lighter. Three days to Bordeaux, then two. One of the burghers bartered his coat for enough water for them all. One of the prisoners gave up his shoes. He needed them, but water was life.

A breeze sprang up from the west, and it carried a taste of the sea.

In the early afternoon they crested a hill and looked down on the wide arm of the Garonne River, dotted with islands, stretching to the horizon.

"If we cross, will we be in Spain?" someone

asked. Elenor was surprised that she knew they would still be in France, and that someone else didn't.

Finally, they stopped at a church and found a priest, mass, a blessing.

"Roland split that rock with one slash of his sword," Etienne whispered to Pipeau, during mass. Pipeau turned slowly around to stare at the rock by the door, licking his cracked lips.

"Roland's here?"

"His body is. He's dead, and he's buried here, in this very church."

In the long twilight, they camped by the edge of the water. Half river, half sea, the water was warm and brackish. Elenor taught Guillemette and Pipeau to float, happy to wallow all evening, the water billowing her shift like the sea nettles that swam slowly by. Marthe borrowed a needle from one of the nuns, a sharp knife from a student, and remade one of Elenor's divided skirts. She cut away the extra cloth of the legs and used it to make the skirt longer and fuller at the bottom. When Elenor tried it on, Guillemette clasped her hands.

"Oh, Nora! You look so tall and beautiful!"

Elenor danced Guillemette around the fire,

whirling barefoot in her new skirt, sending long shadows dancing.

"Now tell us about Roland," Pipeau begged Etienne, as they lay on their backs and watched the sparks from the fire fly into the night sky.

The air was gentle by the river. The fire kept insects at bay. Even Marthe was willing to sleep outside with her children, as long as they all stayed close together. Guillemette lay curled up in the crook of Elenor's arm. Elenor welcomed the story: she did not want to think about reaching Bordeaux. She watched Etienne, the play of firelight accentuating his mobile face, his mop of curly hair, his long, lively hands.

"Charlemagne, Christian emperor of the Franks, is old. His beard flows as white as apple blossoms," Etienne began. "He is tired of fighting.

"For seven years Charlemagne has fought the Moors, and the strongest of his warriors is his nephew Roland. They have rescued all of Spain from the Moors, all except Saragossa, on its mountaintop, where Marsile, king of the Moors, still reigns.

"In Saragossa, there is a shady garden, where Marsile reclines among his lords.

"'How do we get rid of Charlemagne?' asks Marsile.

"His counselor, twirling his black mustache, replies, 'Offer him rich gifts: gold and silver, lions, bears, and camels. Lie to him. Tell him you will accept the Christian faith if he withdraws to France.'

"Marsile's messengers are sent to Charlemagne. On ten white mules they set out, olive branches in their hands.

"In a garden in Córdoba, beside a wild rose tree, they find Charlemagne playing chess with Roland.

" 'What do you think?' Charlemagne asks his counselors.

" 'Do not trust Marsile,' says Roland. 'Carry on with the war!'

"Charlemagne sits with eyes lowered, silently stroking his beard. He longs to return to France.

"Ganelon, Charlemagne's third in command, disagrees: 'Marsile has offered to be your vassal, holding all Spain as his fief. We should not refuse.' Other knights agree. They think that Roland loves war too much.

" 'Let us seal a treaty with Marsile,' says Charlemagne. He signs Ganelon with the cross, and hands him the staff and letter for Marsile. Ganelon puts golden spurs on his heels and rides with Marsile's messengers.

"In Saragossa, Ganelon finds King Marsile sitting in the shade on a throne draped with silk. And

Ganelon the traitor says to the king of the Moors, 'Send a great army to hide in the woods of the pass at Cize. Let the first part of Charlemagne's army go through the pass. Then when only the rear guard is left on the Spanish side of the mountains, attack. Roland will die. With Roland gone, Charlemagne will never gather his might again. In this way we shall all have peace.'

"In Córdoba, Charlemagne awaits news of his messenger. In the early morning, Ganelon arrives. Bugles resound throughout the army. The Franks strike camp; they take the road toward France."

Etienne looked around at his listeners. Thomas had slipped away to gather more wood. Guillemette had drifted off to sleep. Elenor covered her with a cloak.

"You don't like this story, do you, Etienne," she said softly, half questioning.

Etienne shifted from his storytelling posture, looking surprised. "Let me tell it first," he said, "as it is always told." He smiled at her vaguely, as if about to explain something, but Pipeau sat bolt upright, and said impatiently, "I want to hear about Roland fighting."

Elenor watched Etienne take a deep breath and plunge back into the story, and wondered at the way he could weave it like a tapestry and yet stand aloof from judgment.

"By the next day the Franks are at the foot of the mountains. 'Here is the pass,' calls Charlemagne. 'Who shall lead the rear guard?'

" 'Roland!' is Ganelon's prompt reply. 'You have no baron more valiant than he.' Roland does not hesitate to accept the post. His best friend Oliver and the other peers rally to his side.

"The hills are high, the valleys plunged in shadow. Charlemagne and the army leave Roland in the Spanish pass. But heading north, Charlemagne is full of dread, his dreams troubled by strange omens.

"In Saragossa, Marsile summons a hundred thousand soldiers. They don their mailed hauberks, lace their helms, gird on their swords of Viana steel, and take up their shields and lances. Pennants flutter. A thousand bugles sound.

"From a hilltop Oliver sees the sun gleaming on pagan arms. He calls to Roland, 'Sound your horn, so that Charlemagne will hear and turn back.'

"Roland refuses. 'Should I act like a fool and lose my reputation for bravery?'

"Oliver replies, 'I have seen Saracens swarming over every hill and valley. Our men are few beside them.'

" 'That's how I like it,' says Roland.

"In a cloud of dust, the battle is joined. With his lance Roland strikes fifteen blows before its shaft is shattered. Then he draws his sword Durendal and rides at a Saracen prince. He splits his helmet with its gleaming carbuncles, cuts through the cap beneath, down through the head between the eyes, through the shining hauberk and the whole body's length, through the saddle with its beaten gold, and down through the horse's chine before the force of the blow is spent.

"Nor is Oliver idle. The shaft of his lance is broken, but with the stump Oliver knocks a pagan's eyes and brains from his head. Roland sees him.

" 'Companion, where is your sword?'

"Oliver replies, 'I am much too busy striking blows to draw it!'

" 'This is the friend I know!' Roland laughs. 'The emperor loves us for blows like that!'

"The comrades and their knights fight on. The hillsides are covered with dead; those who are alive struggle grimly. In faraway France tempests blow, hailstones hurtle from the sky, and the entire land quakes.

"Roland sets his oliphant to his lips and gives a blast so powerful that it is heard thirty leagues away. Charlemagne hears it, with all his company. 'This is Roland's horn. He is in battle.'

"The emperor rides back toward Spain in wrath and fear, praying for Roland's safety.

"All of his companions are dead. Roland fights on, his body bathed in sweat, and a great aching in his head. Roland feels death's grip closing on him. He takes his sword Durendal, meaning to break it against a rock so that it will never be used by an Infidel. He strikes a nearby rock with all his might, and the rock is split in two.

"Roland lies down with his sword beneath his body. Saint Michael and the cherubim bear his soul up to paradise."

Silence was broken only by the popping of the campfire. Pipeau was still upright, but swaying.

"Did the emperor Charlemagne find Roland?" he asked in a faint croak.

"Yes. Charlemagne found Roland and Oliver and all the army, dead. He brought the bodies back to France. He had Roland buried in the church where we were this afternoon."

"He brought the rock there, too?"

"Yes, the rock, too."

"And the sword Durendal?" Pipeau yawned, tears in his eyes.

"The sword, too."

"And what happened to the bad man?"

"To Ganelon?"

"Yes. What happened to Ganelon?"

"Bad things. He was killed for being a traitor."

"Oh," said Pipeau, with a sigh of satisfaction. "Good-night."

"Good-night," they all said. Elenor snuggled

down next to Guillemette. *What a chump Roland was,* she thought. *I wish Pipeau didn't admire him so. Ganelon was a traitor, but it was he who wanted peace....* Then she was asleep.

"I don't see why everyone thinks he's a hero," Elenor said, as they traveled, next morning, upriver toward the crossing. She mimicked Roland, saying pompously, "The emperor will love me for this: *whack*!"

"He was plain stupid not to call for help when he needed it," said Marthe. "He made the other knights die, too, just so he could be a hero."

Elenor pretended not to notice Pipeau's scowl.

"Why are heroes men?" Guillemette asked. "Why aren't ladies heroes?"

"All heroes aren't men," said Thomas. "What about the Loathsome Lady?" He put his hand over his heart, and grinned at Elenor. "Send me, Loathsome Lady, to the ends of the earth."

"But," said Elenor, blushing, "if she sent you, you would still be the hero." She thought about this. "In stories the men are heroes because of what they do, but if the women are heroes at all, it is because of what they think, or because of what happens to them."

She glanced over to Thomas to see if he was listening. He was.

‡ 175 ‡

"The Loathsome Lady was wise. Does being wise make you a hero?" she asked.

"Not if anybody as dumb as Roland can be one," said Marthe.

Guillemette laughed.

"Nobody has answered your question, though," Elenor said to her, crossing her arms around the child. "Your mother is a hero."

Marthe shifted the baby, Jean-Paul, from one shoulder to the other, ever walking.

"Have you heard the story of Patient Griselda?" asked Etienne.

Thomas groaned. "Yes. And once was enough."

"Tell it!" said Elenor, Marthe, and Guillemette together.

"As you wish," said Etienne.

"You'll be sorry," Thomas said.

Etienne threw back his head, blue eyes sparkling under lowered lids.

"On the shores of Italy," he began, lapsing into a singsong voice, "is a rich plain, ruled over by a lord named Walter, who refuses to take a wife. All of his subjects beg him to marry so that their land will be inherited in peace, but Walter cannot find the perfect woman.

"Not far from the noble palace is a poor village where an old man lives who has one daughter, Griselda, fair and gentle. Walter, riding by, notices

Griselda with serious awareness: her womanliness and goodness commend themselves to him. He asks his barons to prepare a wedding feast, without telling them who the bride will be.

"On the day of the ceremony, Walter rides to the old man's hut.

" 'Will you have me for a son-in-law?' he asks.

"The old man is astounded and stands there deep red and quaking, barely able to nod. Then Walter speaks to Griselda. He asks her to promise to obey his lightest whim and never to offer him any defiance."

"Ehhhhhh?" Marthe broke in.

"Don't do it, Griselda," Elenor muttered.

"Griselda agrees," Etienne said with a serene smile, and continued with his hand on his heart:

" 'Lord,' Griselda answers, 'unworthy though I be of such an honor, if it seems good to you it is to me. I promise never to disobey you in deed or thought.'

"Walter has Griselda dressed in fine clothes and brought to the palace, where they are wed in splendor. With her grace and wisdom Griselda helps Walter advance the public good, and there is peace and prosperity in the land."

Elenor, discouraged, caught Thomas watching her and crossed her eyes. Etienne continued.

"In due course Griselda bears Walter a daughter

dearly loved by her mother. But Walter is seized by a mad passion to try Griselda's constancy. While the child is yet at breast, he tells his wife that he has decided to get rid of the girl. Griselda answers, 'My child and I are your possession. Do therefore as you will.' She marks the child with a cross and a kiss, and gives her over to Walter's henchman. Walter sends the child to be raised by his sister, but lets Griselda think her dead. Griselda never speaks her daughter's name again, and loves Walter as before."

"No-oh!" Elenor interrupted. "This is a revolting story."

"She's not a hero, she's a foot-scraper," said Marthe.

"You wouldn't let anyone take me away, would you, Ma?" Guillemette asked.

"Of course not."

"Do you want to hear any more?" asked Etienne agreeably.

"No," said Marthe.

"Tell more," said Guillemette.

"Make it short," Elenor said.

"I can't," said Etienne, with dignity. "I have to tell it well or not at all. If you want a truncated story, ask Thomas."

They all looked at Thomas.

"Truncated. Let's see. Griselda bears a son. Walter takes the son away. Griselda smiles. Walter tells her he is tired of her."

"Hear, hear," said Elenor.

"Walter makes Griselda his chambermaid, and the whole palace is prepared to receive a new bride for Walter. Griselda scrubs floors, cheerful as ever."

Marthe hissed.

"The new bride arrives, splendidly arrayed, very young. She looks exactly like Griselda did in her radiant youth."

"The daughter! *No!* Not even horrible Walter can marry his own daughter!"

"With the girl comes her brother, now grown into a fine young lad. Griselda wishes Walter much joy, and finally he is overcome with emotion. He introduces his wife to her own children, she swoons in piteous joy, they patch it all up and live happily ever after."

Marthe spat in disgust.

"Is Griselda good?" asked Guillemette.

"She is presented as a hero because of her constancy," said Etienne noncommittally.

"What's the use of being constant if you are constantly a sap?" asked Marthe.

"She overdid it," Elenor explained to Guillemette.

"Roland was a hero in bravery, but a boor in pride," remarked Thomas.

"The Greeks, who valued moderation, would have considered both Roland and Griselda monsters," Etienne declared to the sky.

"I agree with the Greeks, then," said Elenor. "Come on, Guillemette, old girl. It's our turn to walk."

19

Possessions

Old Fra Pietro stopped, bent over for breath, and clung tightly to his human crutches, Elenor on one side, Marthe on the other. He rubbed Elenor's hand, which was tucked under his arm, supporting him.

"Possessions, my girl, are heinous—distracting us from the true—" These few words put him out of breath again. Elenor unplugged her gourd and offered him a sip of water, which he took gratefully, though his hands shook, sending water running down his chin. Elenor looked ahead to where the rest of the pilgrims had disappeared in a cloud of dust. Thomas had asked her to walk with Fra Pietro, to help him keep the pace, but short of putting him on her back, there was no way she could make him hurry.

The old man talked on, in a voice singsong and uneven as the lope of a lame donkey. "A man asked Saint Francis if it would be a sin to own a missal.

Saint Francis told him, 'Buy a missal if you like, but it will make things hard for you. Once you have the missal, you will want a lectern to put it on. Then you will need a table for the lectern, and . . . a roof over the table, to protect it from the weather.' " The friar laughed with a wheeze. Marthe patted him on the back and they stopped again.

Elenor wondered if she had done wrong to buy Thomas a book. She knew he liked it. He carried it in his pocket and sometimes got her to help him read from it. She had been astounded to find that she could read better than Thomas and was glad he was not too proud to ask for her help.

Thomas settled disputes, found people who could help each other, dealt with the constant need for food and lodging, drew on his scant knowledge of Latin to talk with the Italians and Occitans who were now joining them. These were challenges that made him feel sharp and alive, like a juggler.

At present he needed to get sixty people and a horse across the broad arm of the sea to Bordeaux. The boatmen who crowded round plucking at the pilgrims' clothes exuded dishonesty. Thomas called Etienne, who had a gift for the local parlance.

"What are they asking for passage?"

"Anywhere from a penny to four pence, depending on the look of the passenger, and they'll try to squeeze six in a boat."

"Offer a penny each, two for towing the horse, and tell them no more than four to a boat, two if the horse is in tow. The horse will be safer swimming behind a boat with a lead on than trying to stand in a flatboat."

Etienne raised his eyebrows. "And if the boatmen don't agree?"

"Tell them we'll take the whole caravan upriver to another crossing. Tell them I have a map."

"Liar!"

Thomas laughed. "In my head."

Elenor and Marthe sat on the bank with the other women and children. Elenor looked at the small, unstable ferryboats and wished she had worked harder at teaching Pipeau and Guillemette to swim. Pipeau would manage; he wasn't afraid of water and knew enough to dog-paddle. Guillemette could float on her back but hated to get water on her face. Elenor pulled the two spare shirts from her satchel and Thomas' and tied knots in the arms, thinking to use them as floats for the children if the boat went over.

Her eyes scanned the river. Far from shore, there were graceful, seaworthy boats, low in the middle but with high curving bow and stern. "Who rides in those?"

One of the Germans answered, "Those ships carry the wine in the big barrels."

"Where are they carrying it?"

"Out to the ships that go across the sea to England, and to Flanders."

"And where do the ships from England tie up?"

"In Bordeaux, also, but to the west where the water is deep."

Elenor gave Guillemette a squeeze. "That would be close to where your father works. Soon you will see your father again!"

A woman who had recently joined the caravan attracted a crowd, telling fortunes in melodramatic whispers, her wide blue eyes startlingly beautiful in her solemn, weathered face.

"May I?" begged Guillemette. "May I please get my fortune told?"

"No," said Elenor, because Father Gregory had maintained that fortune-telling was flirting with the devil. But Elenor watched in fascination. Was the woman plucking premonitions out of the air, or receiving them from some being only she could see?

Marthe said suddenly, "Watch the children!" She thrust Jean-Paul into Elenor's lap and scrambled down the bank toward the fortune-teller.

Elenor strained to listen, but she couldn't hear the words. She caught a stiffening of Marthe's spine as if a shiver had gone through her, a wild look from the fortune-teller, a little moan from the crowd. Marthe came back very pale. She refused to answer Guillemette's questions, took Jean-Paul back, and hugged him fiercely.

Just then they were called to get into boats.

Comfortable lodgings, only a penny a night!"
"No fleas, no vermin, just good home cooking!"

"Had enough of hard abbey floors? Come to my house and sleep on a feather mattress!"

The wharf at Bordeaux was bustling with people vying for the pilgrims' coins. A few of their company allowed themselves to be hustled away, but most waited in tired groups for Thomas' direction. He looked for and found a Benedictine friar, who led them toward a hospice.

"Where's m' father?"

"Do you see him yet?"

"Is that him?"

Pipeau and Guillemette were flying high with excitement. Marthe was subdued. Elenor walked beside her and lightly put a hand on her shoulder.

"Can I carry Jean-Paul?"

Marthe didn't answer, but held the baby more tightly.

"What's the matter?"

Marthe shrugged. "I don't want to talk about it."

"What did the creepy fortune-teller say?" Elenor asked, losing patience. Marthe hissed, and tears came to her eyes.

"That viper! She said my man had gone off with another woman, and I'd have to find me a new one! She said my life stretched ahead of me like a high, rocky mountain, nothing but trouble!"

Marthe's usually straight shoulders slumped. She looked suddenly old and tired, she who had been so staunch and brave all these days of travel.

They were at the gates of the hospice, filing in one by one. The Brothers waited with bowls to wash the feet of the pilgrims. Elenor ran the back of her finger across Jean-Paul's cheek. He was filling out again, and she was rewarded with a drooly smile.

"As soon as this is done, we'll go find him," she said to Marthe. "No matter what, he will be proud you came so far to see him."

Marching first to the town hall, then to a street where they were directed, Marthe had a white blank look, like a prisoner being led to the gallows. She held Jean-Paul so tightly that he cried, and even Pipeau and Guillemette fell quiet. When they finally reached the door to which they had been sent, it was Elenor who knocked, saying to the children, "Cheer up, or your pa won't recognize you."

The door was opened by a matronly woman. Elenor breathed a sigh of relief and saw a little color coming back into Marthe's face. "Is there a man from Paris named Jean-Loup who lives here?"

"Aye, and would you be the young wife he's been waiting for so long?"

Marthe seemed unable to speak, but Elenor shoved her forward into a smothering embrace. The woman could hug and shout at the same time, and bellowed, "Jean-Loup!"

Jean-Paul howled, and Pipeau pulled on the woman's apron. "Where is he, where is my father?"

Just then an overgrown elf, a bigger version of Pipeau, bounded from behind the house and grabbed his wife away from his landlady. Guillemette let go of Elenor's hand and burrowed in between her parents, while Pipeau climbed his father's leg. Jean-Loup shouted with joy; Pipeau's voice squeaked like a flute; the baby screamed louder than ever and was rescued by Elenor, who wondered why tears were running down her own face.

Even a whiff of the sea was exhilarating after their long overland travels. It made Thomas restless, filled him with energy. He watched the greedy, raucous sea gulls wheeling overhead, and thought of the vision Elenor had told him about, when she had become a bird. *She wouldn't be a gull ... a sparrow maybe, a wild goose, a cuckoo sometimes. ...* He knocked around the Bordeaux wharves, lending his strength to the work being done, helping to roll huge barrels of wine from warehouse to barge, pulling ropes, watching the ships load and unload, talking to sailors from here and there.

A ship no bigger than the *Lady Elwyse* came limping slowly into port, drawing a crowd of gawkers to the wharf. The mast was broken and spliced, the sails badly patched, and some of the rigging missing. The deck was crowded with emaciated people in dark clothes. As Thomas helped the sailors tie up, the passengers' yellow hands clutched the rail like bird claws. Most were unable to walk on land, legs folding suddenly under them. Some Brothers from the hospice were on hand to catch them, crutches and stretchers piled near at hand. Thomas stood by to see if he would be needed, and was relieved to find he wasn't. He was tired of walking slowly, bent over, supporting the old and feeble.

One man who got off with the pilgrims seemed a little stronger than the rest. Thomas hailed him, asked where he was from and if he'd care to share a cup of wine.

"Wine country, is it?" the man answered with a grin. He moved with an uncertain elderly gait from being long at sea. "I'd be glad to toast us all for surviving the trip on that rotten little vessel—bless her heart," he added, turning to take his hat off to the sorry ship.

"You've come far?" asked Thomas.

"From Yarmouth, England, if you know where that is."

Thomas laughed. "I could've sworn that was a sister ship to the *Lady Elwyse*."

"Sir," said the man, "that *is* the *Lady Elwyse*!"

"Then you're here by miracle," said Thomas, and they introduced themselves. The man was Martin McFeery, a Highlander. In Thornham, the Scots were regarded as faraway savages, and not far enough away, at that. In Bordeaux, this Martin McFeery seemed like a brother.

"So ye've come overland all the way from Le Havre," said Martin. "We must compare voyages."

An hour later, over a third cup of wine, Martin McFeery was heard to say, "In short, it was the damn most terrifying experience of me long lifetime, and I'd not do it again for all the gold of Prester John, nor yet for a hundred years off purgatory."

"You'll be joining us, then?" said Thomas.

"Aye, me and probably another sixty knock-kneed, seasick critters."

Elenor took her time thinking over what she would say to Thomas, but when he finally came back to the hospice, he was swaying on his feet, his arm over the shoulder of a lanky Scotsman, singing drunkenly. She decided to let Thomas sleep it off before she tried any serious talking.

Next morning, they went out together to comb Mab. They worked her over, one on each side, in companionable silence.

"You know how much I love this horse," Elenor stated at last.

"I do," said Thomas. "Why else would we be out here so early in the morning, and me with my head splitting?"

"I want to—to sell her," she said in a rush. Thomas stood back in amazement, forgetting his headache.

"Why?"

"We found Jean-Loup. He is living with an old woman—she is a rock, you would like her—but her daughter is marrying and she needs the room that Jean-Loup is living in and so now they need a house, and I found a perfectly beautiful cottage, well, a good cottage, like Sybille's, and it would be perfect for them, but I know that they have no money—" To Thomas' confusion, in the middle of her enthusiasm, she burst into tears. She turned and leaned her forehead against the rough wood of the wall, knocking it gently in mortification. Thomas was horrified. He felt as if it were his head being knocked. He went over and held her by the shoulders, making her stop.

"You don't really want to do it, do you?" he asked gently.

"No." She bent down and blew her nose on her underskirt. "And yes. And it was all my idea. The others know nothing about it. But I want them to have—a place."

"I have a little money left. . . ."

"Not enough money, I think. No one was expecting you to buy a house."

"I think that's true, although I've never tried to buy a house."

"It's a very little house," said Elenor, "on a very little holding; but there is room for a garden, and there are two trees, a chestnut and an apple."

"Shall I do it today?" asked Thomas.

20

Martin

E lenor slapped at a mosquito, smearing blood across her face, and blinked salty sweat out of her eyes. She wrung briny water from her skirt and pushed the hem of it into her waistband to keep it out of the marsh. Another day of slogging through knee-deep water. Her cloak was rolled and tied to her satchel, and her back felt twisted from the weight of it, no matter how she shifted. Gulls wheeled overhead, and an occasional solitary blue heron winged across the sky unhurriedly, alighting on long legs to stalk about poking at shellfish in the brackish water.

Bordeaux was behind them. Marthe and Guillemette, Pipeau and Jean-Paul and Jean-Loup were all together under one roof, with a garden already half-dug, a milk goat, and clothes, washed at the river, drying in the sun. Elenor missed Guillemette most of all; missed having a hand in hers and missed the child's gentle, persistent curiosity.

They had reached a part of the country different from any they had seen, flat, open, and marshy, with patches of brilliant green grass, areas of soft mud and sparagrass, and stretches of shallow water. The air shimmered with insects, and the insects brought birds of many kinds. In the drier areas sheep grazed. When Elenor saw her first shepherd she stopped dead still in amazement. The shepherd was perched on stilts tied to his legs; he moved about with awkward grace, like a heron. She turned to Guillemette to show her, and remembered that Guillemette wasn't at her side.

Elenor gave a big sigh. The children could not have made this part of the journey. Mab might have broken her leg in this uncertain bog. Thinking of Mab's fuzzy face made her ache, as if she were carrying a stone around in her chest. She had not been so sad for a long, long time, but the sadness she felt now, missing Mab, missing Guillemette, seeped into an old sadness like spreading water. She found herself back on the day her little sister was born at Ramsay, a day of light and shadow, joy first, and then words that hit like stones: "You can't go to Mama, Ellie, because she isn't with us anymore." For nothing, because the little sister had died, too.

Guillemette was a good little sister. Mab was a horse you could hug and talk to. Elenor missed them all, cried for them all in a salty wash of complete misery. She had to blink and splash and blink again to see where she was going.

Elenor's heavy sandals grew heavier with mud and water until it no longer seemed possible to drag each one out, to lift it once again for another step. She took them off, squishing her toes in the soft salt mud. Soon the stobs of broken-off sparagrass, the jagged broken shells of tiny razorback clams cut her feet. At first she welcomed the pain. It distracted her and it revived her tears. Then she started to feel sick and dizzy. She had to take hold, or she would just sink down, down. Water, silt, mud, shell, then what? She imagined herself being sucked down, then spewed below into the arms of gleeful devils, chanting as they had done in Peterborough:

> *Eternal remorse, eternal remorse.*
> *The song of the damned is eternal remorse.*

Elenor splashed water over her face, shook herself, scraped her feet, and forced them back into wet sandals. Straightening up, she noticed a person crouched over a little away from the main line of wading pilgrims. *I wish people would go farther off the Way to piss,* she thought, irritated, but she looked again, arrested by the hopeless immobility of the woman. With a sigh, she turned and slogged back across the too-bright water to see what was the matter.

Hunkering in the mud was Melinda, the fortune-teller who had scared Marthe so badly. The light reflected off the water onto Melinda's face, showing blue circles under her eyes like bruises. Melinda did not look up at Elenor's approach. She was staring into space, rocking slightly, humming to herself.

"Melinda! Get up, woman. This is no place for a rest," said Elenor sharply.

Melinda opened her mouth as if to speak, but no sound came out. She licked her parched lips. Elenor waited impatiently, hearing at last a hoarse whisper: "I can't...can't go on..." *Deathbed drama,* thought Elenor. *If I can, you can.* She felt her mouth twist in a sarcastic smile as Melinda croaked, "My dying place...here between the mirrors...die here ... can't go to ... what awaits me."

"And what is that, Melinda? What awaits you? Where?"

Melinda gave a shudder, threw her head back, her eyes rolled up so that they looked a startling dead white. Her voice rose in pitch: "The terror! Mists, great dark trees, and slinking between them, an evil death.... Let it come to me here, in the open." Elenor fought off a sick panic. Pity turned to fear, and fear to anger again.

"Get up, you stupid woman!" she yelled, goose-flesh rising on her arms. "You think it's so much fun to terrify us with your creepy premonitions. Now you've terrified your own stupid self. *Nobody* knows what lies ahead! Nobody! Do you hear? Leave your future to God, get up on your feet, and walk!" Glaring at Melinda, Elenor suddenly remembered how she had told Father Gregory she didn't want to marry, didn't want to bear children, didn't want to go forward. "You can't just stop living!" she shouted. She grabbed Melinda by the forearms, struggling to pull her to her feet, booting her up with a muddy sandal. But Melinda was far heavier than Elenor, and she wouldn't budge. Her arms were clammy and limp. Elenor straightened, shielded her eyes from the glare, and searched for a helper among the pilgrims struggling along the Way. Where was Etienne? Where was Thomas? Among the tiny figures far ahead she saw one taller than the others.

"Thomas!" she shouted. "We need help here. Come, lend a hand!" Heads turned. She was embarrassed by the bossiness of her voice. A man with a reddish beard started toward them. His feet were tied up in rags, each coated with so much mud it looked like a giant's. His vaguely familiar face wavered in reflected light, showing pale gray eyes with white crow's feet at the corners where he had been squinting or laughing into the sun.

"I'll help, missy. What's the matter? Tired out, is she?"

He got on one side of Melinda and pulled her to her feet, while Elenor stood on the other to keep her from falling over. He didn't hurry her, but kept up a gentle patter of talk about mundane things, and Melinda put one foot in front of the other. Elenor hardly listened. She felt chastened, hearing him accomplish with gentleness what she had failed to accomplish with anger. A breeze sprang up and cooled her cheeks.

She shivered, sweat running cold down under her arms.

The land rose at last beneath their feet. As the sun lowered into a pink haze, they stumbled into a Benedictine abbey, with Brothers skilled in healing arts who put poultices on their cuts, and a cobbler to help them repair and replace broken sandals.

The Scotsman Martin McFeery went out after supper to sit on a hill and watch the sunset, while the other pilgrims settled for the night. On his way back into the hospice he heard the faint sound of someone crying. When he went to investigate, he found the little English girl who was traveling with his new friend Thomas. The same girl, he realized now, who had helped him pull Melinda out of the mud. She was sitting on a stone wall facing a flock of sheep who had been gathered in for the night, her knees pulled up under her chin, her arms locked around them, tears running down her face. Martin sat on the wall beside her and handed her a very dirty rag to blow her nose on.

"Go on," he said. "It can't get any worse."

After a while, he pointed out a sheep with an especially fatuous expression. "I once knew a troubadour who looked like him. I wonder if this fellow knows any love ballads." The sheep opened its mouth, drooped its eyelids, and let out a small belch.

"So what's the trouble?" asked Martin. "Anything you'd care to tell me about?"

"I—" As soon as she started to talk, tears welled up in Elenor's eyes again. "Drat!" she said, swallowing. "I miss my horse."

Thomas came out looking for Elenor and saw her sitting on the wall talking to Martin. He hesitated, then walked the other way. Martin was a decent fellow, but if Elenor was feeling bad, he would rather cheer her up himself.

Martin played a lute, which he carried slung over his shoulder in a big leather bag. He would travel with the caravan for a few hours, loiter at a village, and then catch up running, hours later, often with children pointing and laughing and skipping around him. Sometimes he made them guess what was in his bag, told them wild tales until even the youngest realized he was fooling them, and then sat down and with great ceremony drew out his lute. Then he would get the children to teach him songs.

Thomas didn't try to keep Martin with the other pilgrims.

One hot, hazy afternoon, just as they were beginning to climb the blue foothills of the Pyrenees, Elenor saw Martin's form wavering in the heat, coming her way across a golden field of stubble with his dancing stride, a group of children running alongside. He called her with a yodel he had learned from mountain shepherds. As the echoes bounced from hill to hill, the children rolled around on the grass with glee. Elenor waited until she saw Martin flop down among them and then made her way over.

"Birthday!" shouted Martin.

"Whose?" she shouted back.

"Dah dah dah doot—da doo!" intoned Martin, reaching into his sack. And out came, not the expected lute, but a wriggling ball of fur. "Introducing Greatheart, faithful hound-to-be to the Lady Elenor!"

After a flurry of rushing about, jumping and licking, the pup, of a white, fuzzy, wide-muzzled breed, settled in Elenor's lap as if he knew he had found a home.

21

Astray

Mountains rose all around them, striped purple and golden in the early morning light. The pilgrims climbed cheerfully, strengthened by the Benedictines' bread, wine, and shoe leather. Greatheart bounded among the hills, a spot of creamy white in perpetual motion. Too young to know a rabbit if he met one nose to nose, he had nevertheless inherited from his ancestors wild hunting enthusiasms, and the mere whiff of rabbit had him mad with excitement.

It was one such tantalizing trail that led Greatheart away around the piles of boulders and through a crevasse, out into an adjoining valley, so far away that when he turned to go back to his new friend, he couldn't find her. When he tried to sniff a way to his mother, for milk and comfort, even though he was big for her now and she would nip him, he could not find her, either. After a while he sat down and howled, and then his howling wore down to a whimper, and he circled a few times and curled up and escaped from loneliness into sleep.

Elenor lagged behind the main group of pilgrims, once again holding the arm of the old Italian friar. Fra Pietro was not talking today, too winded by the climb. Elenor listened anxiously to his labored breathing, and missed his stories. She called out from time to time to Greatheart. Sometimes he came. Sometimes he didn't. Calling him gave her something to do. She wished she could change bodies with him, and go bounding off across the hills herself. Martin came back along the Way, whistling.

"I've lost Greatheart," she told him.

"I'll go look for him," Martin offered, but seeing Elenor's expression, he added, "It's yourself should go, though. The dog will come more readily to you. I'll be happy to walk with Fra Pietro."

Elenor went off joyfully, keeping the winding pilgrim path in sight, a reddish path, well-worn, snaking its way up through the pass.

She climbed among the rocks, calling and whistling. She'd only had Greatheart a day; he would hardly know his own name yet. But she thought he would know her voice, if he were calm enough to hear it. She herself listened with all her might. A faint breeze stirred around the mountains, the cool air from the heights meeting the warm breath of the fields, mixing sounds from near and far, a snatch of song or conversation from the pilgrims, the sound of a rock knocked loose and rolling, the bleating of sheep and the tinkling of sheep bells, the sound of hooves over rock. For a moment she thought she heard a dog howling. She stood very still, only turning her head slightly to see if she could catch the sound again. There it was, coming very faintly from across a boulder-strewn ridge, a thin, sad howl. Elenor went off after it. She'd have to run fast to find Greatheart and get back to the Way before she was missed. A quiet internal voice, suspiciously like Father Gregory's, told her she should not let the path out of sight, but she ignored it, running on, jumping now from stone to stone, nimble and free as a goat. Then she hit a loose stone, twisted her ankle, and fell with a head-splitting crash that sent stars shooting through her brain.

She lay very still, cursing her foolishness. *I'm a pack of trouble for everybody now,* she thought. She ran her tongue over her teeth. There was blood in her mouth. Slowly, she tried to raise her head. A wave of nausea washed over her; she felt herself spinning and disappearing, drawn into an intense world of awe and fear. She was in a great hall, hung with red. In the middle sat God in all his glory, surrounded by the saints. God had the face of Father Gregory. Her heart leaped to see him, but she hung back in shame. She had done wrong. She had broken her most sacred vows. She was selfish and a nuisance. She would be cast into hell, through her own wickedness. One of the saints stood forth, defending her before God. It was Saint James—she could recognize him by his strong back and his big hands, with which he gestured as he spoke to God in her defense. He turned his face slightly. It was Thomas' face. Her dream swirled again; she opened her eyes painfully on the bright whiteness of the mountain sunshine, and closed them tight, feeling the breeze for a moment against her sweaty forehead before she passed out again.

Mists and ghosts didn't scare Thomas, and he enjoyed ordering Melinda the fortune-teller to keep her dreams to herself. But he dreaded Roncesvalles. The higher they climbed, and the more the mountains closed in, the worse Thomas felt.

Above them in the narrow pass was the battlefield where Roland died. According to the pilgrim guidebook memorized and much quoted by Etienne, it had become the tradition for pilgrims to plant crosses in the pass and to pray for "soldiers of Christ."

Thomas wasn't a bit sure that his prayers made any difference one way or the other, and he had nothing against ordinary soldiers. He walked along thinking of a long and motley parade of men he had known who had the misfortune to make their living as soldiers: jokesters, cowards, bullies, braggarts, even a few humble types who might be described as "Christian." For the first time since childhood, Thomas, unhorsed, felt short, and his lowly position, ever walking in the dust, made him feel like a foot soldier.

But when people used the phrase "soldiers of Christ," it was hard to imagine real live, short, bored soldiers. False images were held up like icons: Roland, on horseback, slashing his sword Durendal down through some man's eyes, neck, body, horse; Saint George, slaying the dragon. To Thomas such soldiers of Christ as Roland represented everything he had been fool enough to admire. Thomas remembered Elenor and Marthe's summary dismissal of Roland and laughed out loud.

He climbed cheerfully for a while, then grew gloomy again. Roland-worship required Moorbashing. Roncesvalles was a place where pilgrimage would turn to crusade. Someone was bound to preach about the treachery of Saracens, Moors, and heathens. In the mummers' plays they'd done as children at Ramsay, it wasn't a dragon Saint George fought, it was the "king of Egypt," a Moor.

There was a mood of excitement among the pilgrims as they stomped their way toward Ronces-valles. *Anticipation,* Thomas thought ruefully. *We are about to celebrate other people's wickedness. If I were smart, I'd think of some way to keep us honest.*

Still, Thomas was dutiful. He took his charge to minister to the pilgrims seriously. He knew that if some of the pilgrims came to the battlefield without crosses to plant, they would feel sad, even guilty. In a copse before the last climb to the battlefield, Thomas sent Etienne to remind people about the tradition, to pass word down the line. They both helped some of the more feeble pilgrims fasten their pine sticks together and helped them carry their prickly crosses when they stumbled on the steep path.

Shadows lapped up toward the battlefield, a deep green covered with hundreds and thousands of crosses, some old and broken and almost rotted back into the earth, many new, made of this year's green pine. With a pointed pole, Thomas helped make holes for the crosses, so that they would stand straight. When all the crosses were planted and the pilgrims knelt looking out over the darkening hills, Thomas saw tears on many faces, and fended off a tenderness for the pilgrims and their fragile hopes.

Fra Pietro's tremulous voice rose like a little wisp of smoke, leading a prayer of dedication followed by muddled references to "the scourge of the Infidel."

In the silence that followed, Thomas looked around in search of someone whom he could encourage to speak next, someone who might find words to draw out the beauty of the moment without putting it to ill use. He looked for Martin to start a song, but Martin was nowhere to be seen.

Thomas was no speechmaker, but he spoke, and was surprised to hear more certainty in his own voice than he felt.

"Let us celebrate together the spirit of the pilgrim who seeks after God, whether the pilgrim be Christian or Moor." A murmur went through the crowd. "Let us say together the Lord's Prayer, as it is written in our Bible, and as it is written, just the same, in the holy book of Islam, and let us say it in every language of which we have a speaker here. Our Father . . ." As the prayer ended in English, he touched the shoulder of one of the Germans, who took it up in his language, followed by Fra Pietro in Italian, a Benedictine in the French of the north, Melinda in the French of the south, a young boy who had just joined them in the tongue of Navarre. . . . While the prayers rolled across the hills, he found Martin, and when the praying lagged, Martin led them in songs of praise.

* * *

In another hour's walk, drawn on by the pealing of bells, the pilgrim convoy was welcomed through the gates of Sancti Spiritus.

There was jubilation among the pilgrims: everywhere Thomas looked, people were laughing, elated. They had passed over into Spain. They were less than twenty days from Santiago. They had planted their crosses and by that gesture made themselves one with the hundreds of thousands of pilgrims who had gone before and who would come after. Fra Pietro babbled to anyone who would listen, tears of joy running down his face. The Brothers of Sancti Spiritus pitched out clean broom straw and ladled up soup. A stream had been dammed so that pilgrims could wash, and the women had gathered there, taking their turn first. Thomas waited, counting the other pilgrims and talking with the Brothers.

"There are still Moors in these mountains," one Brother warned Thomas. "Be sure to tell all your people to stay on the Way. They can't be trusted, you know. Especially around women," he added confidentially.

Thomas suddenly missed Elenor.

When the women pilgrims came back from the bathing place, she was not among them.

"Have any of you seen Nora?"

Melinda looked at Thomas with her wide eyes. "Shall I try for a sighting?" she asked.

"No!" he shouted, suddenly fearful. "No, thank you, Melinda, not now."

He went to find Martin, who was pitching stones with some other men. A clink of stone sounded on iron, and the others grouped around him, cheering and patting him on the back. Thomas pulled him aside.

"When did you last see Nora?"

Martin thought back slowly.

"At the foot of the mountain, midafternoon. She went looking for the dog. . . ."

Thomas was so angry his hands and forehead throbbed. Angry at Martin for letting her go. Angry that Martin should have given Elenor Greatheart in the first place.

"Martin, Etienne, listen," he said, clasping his friends by the shoulders so tightly he would leave bruises. "I am going out to look for her. No, I'll go alone. The Brothers will be ringing nones soon, and then vespers. If we are not back by then, ask them to keep ringing the bells, so that she and I can have a guide. If she comes back before I do, ask them to ring only one bell, in groups of three, so that I will know."

22

Pierre Maury

Pierre Maury watched his sheep pour like water over the hill and down into the ravine, the sun dappling their backs. He counted them automatically, not so much by number as by the size and configuration of the herd. He knew each animal, and knew which would be running close to which. He walked loosely, whistling, enjoying the cool air and swinging his staff. The croak of a raven made him look up, golden brown eyes scanning the sky. It was the call a raven gives when it sees something out of the ordinary, a hurt animal, a glint of metal. Pierre Maury watched for the bird, and saw that it rose above the ravine, a little to the east of the flock.

He walked east, searching the groups of boulders as he went, the crevasses where an animal might catch a leg, the sun-warmed surfaces where a snake might come to warm itself. He looked for anything out of the ordinary, and soon he found what had alarmed the bird. There was a bundle of black cloth down in the dry riverbed where rocks piled one on another. He ran down to it, jumping from rock to rock, and squatted, touching the rags gently. There was a person here. Alive, yes. A girl, by the looks, not conscious. He glanced around. No one else in sight. Perhaps she had strayed off the pilgrim trail; her clothes were such as pilgrims wore. She was no one he knew from Montaillou or from Seb-egues. Her hair was a baked-earth color, but shiny. Most girls here had brown hair, or black, unless they colored it with henna leaves. He put the girl over his shoulder. She was no heavier than a *mar-rane,* a year-old sheep, and he carried her easily.

Elenor woke to a strangely rocking feeling, as if she were on a boat. Then she was lying on something very soft, wooly. A sheep fleece like she had at home. Someone was rubbing a sweet-smelling herb on her back. Someone with strong hands. Thomas? No, it couldn't be Thomas. He was far away with the pilgrims. They must be in Spain by now. She was in the sun. She could feel the warmth of it on her back, on the back of her whole body. Gentle fingers were combing through her hair, picking out fleas. She thought of Carla, and drifted from unconsciousness into the confident sleep of a baby.

As the sun fell lower, Pierre covered up the girl.

He held the back of his fingers against her cheek. No fever. He waited for her to wake up. He felt that she had been sent to him by his good fortune, and he wanted to lie down beside her and make love to her, but she was very young and had many bruises, and he did not want to hurt her. So he waited, and while he waited he built a fire in his oven, made a wrapping of flour and lard and water, and filled it with stew for a pie.

Elenor woke to a good smell, and saw that she was in a small hut made of wattle and daub, such as shepherds use for temporary shelter. In one corner clothes hung on a hook. In another was a mud stove, smoking; a man was bending over it, tending the cooking. She did not know how to tell him she was awake, so she watched him instead. He was young and stocky, and he moved with confidence. She was not afraid of him. She moved a little, to pull the robe up over herself, and he turned and saw her watching him. He smiled and pulled up a stool where she could see him without sitting up. He spoke to her slowly in langue d'oc.

"I am Pierre, a shepherd. I found you in the valley, where you had fallen. Do you hurt?"

Elenor took stock of her body. She felt sore and stiff in places, her knee would barely bend, and there was a lump on her forehead, but she was not much hurt.

"No," she said in French, but imitating his way of speaking as best she could. "I think I am well."

Pierre looked at her very hard. Then he smiled again, a warm and generous smile. "We must speak to each other with our minds," he said. "Our languages are not quite the same." He turned around to check the oven. "Are you hungry?"

"No," said Elenor, meaning not yet. "It has a good smell," she added truthfully, and so as not to sound discourteous.

"And it is not ready," said Pierre, turning to her again.

"Shall we lie together and have joy of our bodies?" he asked, raising his eyebrows slightly.

Elenor laughed out loud in her surprise. *While the pie bakes ...* she thought, and realized to her added surprise that some part of her would like to say yes.

"I might like that, too, but I cannot," she said, shaking her head at the same time, hoping to be understood, trying hard to speak with her mind, as this strange young man had said they must do. "I am a pilgrim. I have taken a vow, and may not ... be joined with anyone."

Pierre looked disappointed. He nodded his head gravely. "This is a big difference between your religion and mine," he said. "In mine we believe that love is good if both people like it, even that it is a gift of God, like the sun."

Elenor remembered how gentle the touch of the sun had been when she awoke before, and the equally gentle touch of fingers in her hair. Perhaps he was right. She thought of Thomas, too. She found she could not talk lightly to this man.

"Are you not then a Christian?"

"Oh, yes. I am a Good Christian." He looked at her with affection and trust. "Do not tell the priests."

She remembered hearing that the Albigensians, those that had been hunted so long for heresy, called themselves Good Christians.

"A—heretic, then?"

Pierre Maury nodded. "It is in my upbringing, and now many die for this." He shrugged and then stretched his arms to the ceiling. "I thought you had been sent to me by my good fortune. And indeed, perhaps you have, though not in the way I had thought."

"Perhaps it is the other way around, and you were sent by my good fortune, so that I should not die in those rocks," said Elenor. "I thank you for bringing me in."

"What is it that you do in the world, that you were born to do?" asked Pierre. "And what are you called?"

"My name is Nora," said Elenor. "And as for what I was born to do—I was born to a lord and lady, who both died. I am to take their place and—help make our village good to live in."

"This village has many troubles?"

Elenor nodded.

"My village, too, has many troubles. Because of the bishop of Toulouse, who makes us pay a tax on every lamb. Because we have beliefs different from the Catholic church, and the Inquisition wishes to know everything, and takes some people away, breaking up our homes." Pierre said this matter-of-factly.

"What happens to those who are taken away?" Elenor wondered.

"They are imprisoned in Carcassonne, or they are burned at the stake," said Pierre. Elenor looked so shocked that he reached out and touched her face, a gesture of reassurance. "It is a trouble, but the world continues." He looked out over the hills, deep in shadows. He glanced back at the girl, who was sitting up now, wrapped in his blanket, hugging her knees. He should not have answered her question, perhaps. She looked as if she herself were feeling the flames of the persecution. "It does not hurt, I've been told. God takes the pain upon himself. We simply do what we must."

"You, too?" she asked.

"Here there is much freedom," he said, and changed the subject, adding, "And in your village, you do not have this trouble?"

"No," said Elenor, never having even imagined the possibility, although now she saw the disagreement between Friar Paul's followers and Father Gregory's in a new light. She saw for the first time why Father Gregory had felt it necessary to make a dramatic gesture of reconciliation toward the Penitents, which had taken the form of this pilgrimage.

Again Pierre waited, seeing that she was lost in thought. Then he asked, "What is it like there?"

"Our troubles are different, although there are also some problems with taxes that are too heavy. Our men were away for a long time, and when they came back, they could not—find their families again. They were like strangers." Elenor had never tried to explain this to anyone.

"Do you, too, belong to a man?" he asked.

"I am betrothed to a man of my home. And will marry if I get back there."

"It is far away?"

"Very far. Fifty, sixty days' walk."

Pierre whistled. "I've been far, but never so far as that. And is your man a stranger to you?"

"He was, but now he is not so much," said Elenor, rocked by a sudden strong pang of affection and longing. "He travels, too, on the pilgrimage."

"With the same vow? The vow not to?" Here Pierre joined the fingers of his two hands. Elenor nodded. Pierre shook his head with a dubious smile.

"And you, will you marry?" asked Elenor, blushing.

"I am a shepherd. I own nothing, and so I will not marry, because you see I could not pay for a house." He looked down for a moment. When he met her eye again, his face was clear. "This is my life, my fate. I have many friends on both sides of the mountains. I sponsor many children in baptism, and sometimes I am even happy in that fortune sends me a woman to share my bed." He smiled at her. "But not you. I understand."

"If I had been given your fate," said Elenor, "I would not be sad, either. And as it is, sometimes I have wished for a different fate, but now I do not."

She only wished there was a way she could tell them that she was safe, that she could make herself not be a nuisance to them, and that she could find Greatheart. "It is a trouble," the shepherd had said, about much worse things, "but the world continues."

She sighed deeply, much as Pierre had done, the kind of sigh that lets go of troubles.

With the cabin door propped open to the sunset, they sat to eat the pie. Pierre crossed himself and drew a little cross on the crust before cutting it with his knife.

"Do other shepherds live here?" Elenor asked. She had noticed two cloaks hanging beside the door.

"There are only two of us this summer. Hassad and me. He will come in later. We will leave some pie for him." His eyes sparkled at her.

The pie had spices and vegetables and eggs in it.

"You cook well. You do not eat meat?" asked Elenor.

"Those of our religion do not eat meat, because"—he stopped to chew and drink water, and then passed the cup with an apology—"we believe that all living creatures have the same kind of soul."

"I think horses have souls," Elenor ventured. "Dogs, too. But not chickens. I'm not sure about chickens or fish."

"A raven showed me where you were, today."

"*Oc,*" Elenor conceded, picking up the langue d'oc way of saying yes, "maybe ravens, too. But I should not be sitting here eating pie. I should be finding the Pilgrim Way, finding the others."

Pierre reached over and touched her shoulder. "Now is the time for pie. Later, we will search. What made Nora get lost? Is not the Pilgrim Way one long road?"

"It is! I was foolish and wanted to find my dog, and to cover being foolish, I hurried, and then, as you saw, I fell. I think a rock jumped up to hit me on the head!"

"There are spirits all around, so thick we bump into them without knowing. Why was Nora hurrying so blindly?"

"There is a pledge we pilgrims make, to help each other, and not to cause difficulties for each other. If I am missed, I am afraid everyone will stop while I am looked for."

"And this dog you are seeking, you love him more than your pledge?"

She told him about Mab and about Greatheart, feeling lighter as she talked. Even though she guessed he did not understand all her words, she felt Pierre understood her. He was silent for a while, and she had the comforting feeling he was thinking over her troubles, yet not too gravely.

"I do know for a fact that horses have souls," he said. "My friend who is both wise and truthful told me a story about this. Would you hear it?"

"Please."

"There was once a man who was a wicked murderer. He died, and his spirit entered the body of an ox. The ox had a harsh master who covered him with scars, but he remembered that he had been a man. When the ox died, his spirit entered the body of a horse. The horse belonged to a lord. One night, the lord was attacked by his enemies. To escape, he jumped on his horse, and rode him fast over rough ground. The horse caught its hoof between two stones; it wrenched it free, but lost its shoe, which remained wedged between two stones. Later, the horse died. Its spirit entered a pregnant woman and inhabited the body of the child she was carrying. When the child grew up, he went walking with his companion, who is my friend. They passed the very place where the horse had lost its shoe. The man, who remembered when his spirit had inhabited the horse, said to my friend, 'When I was a horse, I lost my shoe between two stones near here, and went unshod the whole night.' Then they both began to search among the stones: they found the shoe and took it with them."

Elenor reeled with the effort of following this story, which Pierre related earnestly. The migration of one soul from body to body did not ring true to her, but she tried to understand what it was that Pierre believed.

"How do you suppose the spirit goes from one body to another?" she asked.

"My friend told me—I asked him the same question—" Pierre wrinkled his forehead in concentration: "When the spirits come out of the body that has died, they run very fast, because they are fearful. They run so fast that if a spirit came out of a body on one side of the mountains, and ran to a living body on the other side, if it was raining hard, scarcely three drops of rain would touch it. Running like this, the terrified spirit hurls itself into the first hole it finds free! Into the womb of some animal that has just conceived an embryo not yet supplied with a soul; whether a bitch, a female rabbit, or a mare. Or even the womb of a woman. That is what my friend told me."

"The women must be very careful, then, when they are pregnant," said Elenor. "Think of getting a baby with the spirit of a chicken!"

"Women wear charms sometimes."

His eyes wandered to a piece of wood on a thong, which hung on a peg in the doorway.

"Is that a charm?" she asked.

He took it down and handed it to her. The wood had designs on it, curled writing.

"Is this Arabic writing?" she asked.

"Arabic, Saracen, yes. These are words written down by a Saracen soothsayer, to whom I went to ask about an illness suffered by the sheep of my cousin."

Pierre put his hand on hers as he spoke, pointing out the words, and Elenor, though she liked the feel of his warm skin, lifted the talisman by its thong and handed it back to him.

"Was he a friend, then?"

"He is a man who helps many. He can tell a person's illness from the way the person walks."

"Where does he live?" Elenor was full of excitement. She had never thought to see a Saracen, or to come close to one.

"Why would Nora wish to know such a thing? Do you want him to give you a spell for your bruises? I can do that."

"Oh, you do not need to tell me. I only asked to know that he is real, because in England we only hear of Saracens in stories, and in the stories they are always bad."

"He gave me the spell to tie around the neck of the leader of the flock, and I did it. Later the sheep in the flock who were suffering got well. I keep it in case they become ill again."

Pierre laughed at her look of surprise. "In any case," he continued, watching for her reaction, "Nora need not go so far to meet a Saracen. Hassad is a Saracen, and he lives right here. He is a good man, a fine shepherd. He eats pie like we do."

A half-moon bathed the path and boulders in a tricky light. Thomas was full of foreboding and self-reproach. He should have looked out for Nora. He should have noticed that she wasn't at the battlefield. He forced himself to be truthful; he had noticed her absence at the same time that he had noticed Martin's, and he had deliberately put it out of his mind. Jealousy shamed both Nora and himself. Because he refused to be jealous, or to admit that he could be, he had shoved Nora to the back of his mind, gone about his own way, and now she was lost.

Nora, Elenor, Brat. He almost always thought of her now as Nora, a person halfway between the Brat she'd been and the Lady Elenor she was becoming; Nora, his companion, who liked the same stories, who slept at his back, and was afraid of owls.

The stars were clear and bright, but familiar as they were, they were of no help to him. He wondered if Nora knew how to read the stars, how to find her way by them, and cursed himself when he remembered that he had never told her that from Roncesvalles their path turned west. He prayed, desperately aware that he might be inventing a god out of his own need, and in the absence of an answer realized that his search had to be his prayer. He searched diligently, thoroughly, fooled many times by shadows he thought might be a fallen girl. Before the first light, at the part of the night that seemed darkest because the stars were beginning to fade, he heard a faint tolling of bells. Hope made it hard for him to hear, but he made himself listen calmly. The bells pealed singly, not in threes, though their sounds were jumbled by the hills. Nora had not come back. He searched on, walking farther and farther from the bells.

23

The Saracen

Elenor opened her eyes to see the thick weave of a mud-and-wattle wall. The mountains were vibrating with sound. Her body felt stiff and unfamiliar. For a timeless moment she was an insect inside a woven basket, hearing the mysterious thunder of human voices. Then she came to herself, remembered where she was, and rolled over gingerly to see where the sound was coming from.

Just outside the doorway of the shepherd's hut, facing east toward where the sun, not yet risen, was brightening the sky, a man was on his knees praying. His voice rolled out across the hills, echoing, and his body moved with the song, so that sometimes he was up on his knees, his eyes closed, singing straight into the rising sun, and sometimes bent over with his forehead touching the earth. Though she didn't understand the words, Elenor had no doubt that his song was a prayer of praise.

"Allahu Akbar! La ilaha il-Allah, Muhammad-un Rasulu-llah! Allahu Akbar!"

Elenor caught the name of Muhammad. She looked questioningly at Pierre, who was kneading bread dough, tearing off wads of it, and forming small loaves. He gave her a nod in greeting and put a finger to his lips. Elenor got up stiffly, quietly tried to make herself neat, and straightened the sheepskin and blanket. When the prayers were over, Hassad rose, brushed the grass off his knees, and came into the hut. He was taller than Pierre and had to duck his head coming through the doorway.

"Hassad, this is Nora, who is a Christian pilgrim."

Hassad put his palms flat on his thighs and bowed, so Elenor did the same. Then she slipped outside to find some privacy, her heart pounding. She had met a real Saracen! She would have breakfast with him! What would she say? Would she have the courage to imitate Pierre Maury and simply ask, "What are you in this world to do?"

Hassad had the same golden tawny-colored eyes as Pierre, and dark skin, and he tore off bites of bread with white teeth; two of the front ones were missing. He talked even while he ate, chewing and swallowing and talking, the muscles working in his strong brown neck. Amulets swung in the opening of his shirt: a little pouch, a shell, and a stamped metal hand.

"You woke to find me at my prayers! Were you surprised? These are the praises of Allah, which we sing five times every day. *Allahu Akbar!* It means ..."

He looked at Pierre with his eyebrows raised, and Pierre filled in, "God is most great."

"Allahu Akbar," said Elenor carefully. "Is this the—real God? The one true God?"

"Yes. Of course. That is what we say next: *la ilaha il-Allah,* there is no God but Allah."

Elenor looked at Pierre anxiously, not knowing how to ask her question inoffensively. In her mind every Saracen had a cutlass at his belt, ready for use at the least insult, and Allah was a foreign term.

"Nora means, I think," said Pierre, "is Allah the same god as the Christian God?"

Hassad chewed and swallowed before answering. He smiled at Elenor, and said, "There is only one God, the Almighty, the All-Merciful. We call him Allah, as you call him God, but we do not see how you Christians can call him one and yet also three."

Elenor felt her ears get red. She had never had to explain the Christian faith to anyone outside of it.

"It is a mystery," she said. "The Trinity is a mystery."

"God the All-Powerful is mystery enough," said Hassad. "Since God is All-Encompassing, he does not need to be three. He is not like"—he gestured toward the sheepfold—"sheep, who are one flock but many animals."

"Wait," said Elenor, laughing. "I am lost. How do you say, 'There is no God but God?'"

"*La ilaha il-Allah.* Try it." He laughed at her hesitation. "It will not make you a bad Christian."

Elenor tried the words. She liked the sound and the feel of them.

"*La ilaha il-Allah.* And the part about Muhammad?"

"Do you know already about Muhammad? This part says *Muhammad-un Rasulu-llah*: Muhammad is his prophet."

"Is Muhammad to you what Jesus is to us?"

"Muhammad is the founder of Islam. Jesus is the founder of Christianity. But there is a difference, because we do not believe that Muhammad is God. We do believe in Jesus, that he was a very great prophet, but we do not believe he was God, either." Hassad took the cup and filled it from a bucket. He drank deeply, and handed it to Elenor. "Talk is making me thirsty, not you?"

Elenor thanked him and drank. She was feeling braver now. "May I ask you one more question?"

"Please, yes," said Hassad.

"What is the religion they call—Islam?"

Hassad threw back his head and laughed, while Pierre looked on, content to leave the sheep in the fold for a little while more.

"That is one big question! But luckily not so difficult, because the Angel Gabriel asked Muhammad the same question, and his answer I have learned by heart at my mother's knee."

As Hassad spoke, he held up one hand, counting off on his fingers one by one. "Islam is"—he grasped his thumb—"to read the words of Allah and his prophet"—he touched his pointing finger next—"to pray, as I was praying this morning; to give alms; to fast; and to make the pilgrimage." He shook his strong brown hand in the air, fingers outspread. "These five things, these are the practice of Islam: study, prayer, alms, fasting, pilgrimage."

He got to his feet and stretched and smiled. "So you see it is not so difficult. When I come in from the sheep, I will ask you, 'What is Christianity?'" He smiled. "And Nora will be ready for me, and explain all about this three-in-one, and not just say to me, 'It is a mystery.'"

He picked up a tall crook that stood against the wall, and ran down to the sheepfold, skipping from rock to rock as Elenor had tried to skip the day before, practiced and graceful in his movements. Pierre watched Nora watch Hassad.

"And now what does Nora think of Saracens?" he asked.

"Nora thinks she has much to learn about the world," she replied.

"I have heated some water for you," said Pierre, "and while you bathe your scratches, I will see to my sheep. If they are well, I will go with you to find this dog of yours, and to find the way to the hospice of Sancti Spiritus. There you will surely find your fellow pilgrims." Pierre still spoke slowly, looking at her intently so that she would understand him.

She answered in surprise, "Thank you for your help, Pierre, and I hope you find your sheep well. But isn't Sancti Spiritus in Spain?"

Pierre looked at her quizzically. "This side of the mountain is Spain, what is sometimes called the kingdom of Navarre. The sheep do not know the difference, nor do I."

"Pierre."

"Yes, Nora?"

"Did Hassad say the Angel Gabriel spoke to Muhammad?"

A pained expression briefly crossed Pierre's face. "Yes."

"The same Angel Gabriel that spoke to Zacharias, and to the Blessed Mother Mary?"

"I think so, yes."

"Then why don't Christians consider Muhammad a prophet, too?"

Pierre shook his head. "Perhaps Nora will find out on her pilgrimage. But now the water becomes cold." He picked up his staff and bounded away, leaving Elenor to bathe.

24

Contradance

Greatheart came from a long line of sheepdogs. The rainlike drumming of hooves on rock, the gentle tinkling of sheep bells stirred his blood like a clarion call. These were the sounds he awoke to, his nose twitching to the smell of warm wool and manure.

Hassad was in a good mood. He was singing a song about a girl from the Wadi Hammamat, who was as beautiful as a green parakeet. Hassad had never seen either the Wadi Hammamat or a green parakeet; the song was one his grandfather had sung, and he liked the way it trilled and curled in the air, its loops and curlicues of sound. It was a song you could sing all day and not get tired of it. While Hassad sang of the girl from Wadi Hammamat, he thought about the little Nora whom Pierre had found, and hoped that she would stay with them awhile. He would make a good

Muslim of her, maybe then a girlfriend or wife. He imagined bringing her into his grandfather's garden, where his grandfather sat to smoke with the men in the cool of the evening. The other women of the household would be peeping out to see this new woman, curious and whispering to each other, but out of sight behind the leaves. Nora would follow Hassad, bowing respectfully to Grandfather, her hands on her knees. And Grandfather would see the color of her hair, and say, "Oh! But she is a Christian!" and Hassad would say, "No, Grandfather, not anymore. I have taught her well." Then Grandfather would say, "Speak, child," and Nora would recite twenty suras flawlessly, and the women behind the leaves would coo and applaud gently, and the breeze would shake the leaves, joining the applause. . . .

Hassad's reveries were interrupted by a mad puppy, who came catapulting over the ridge of a hill and dashed straight toward the shepherd, scattering frightened sheep to either side, leaping on Hassad's chest, tail wagging, tongue licking. Hassad was not fond of dogs. He shouted in surprise. He tried futilely to calm the animal, and set about trying to round up the excited, bleating sheep. The sound of this commotion, echoing in the quiet of the morning, woke Thomas, who had been searching the rocks near the Way all night, and had fallen asleep at dawn, worn out by climbing up and down hills and by the intensity of his wish for Elenor. Thomas jumped to his feet. Greatheart ran a wide circle and headed for this new, vaguely familiar person. Hassad raised his arms to heaven, shouting in Arabic, *"Hamd'Allah!* He has sent me another Christian pilgrim!"

Yaar! She's gone," said Hassad. He and Thomas peered into the little cabin. It was empty, its door held neatly open on leather hinges by a stone.

"Pierre must have gone with her to take her to the trail of pilgrims." He grimaced and shook his head. "Why was she in such a hurry to leave? It was good to have her here. Good to have a person to talk to. You! You could have stayed, too. Tonight the girl was going to tell me what I asked her . . . which I think she could not do . . . to tell me in few words what is Christianity."

Thomas was looking curiously at the cabin where Elenor had slept, admiring the neat simplicity of it, the oven, the amulet by the door, the leather hinges. Hassad recaptured his attention by punching him in the arm.

"Can you tell me?"

Thomas felt weak-kneed with gratitude at learning that Nora was alive, and clearheaded but slow from lack of sleep. He wished Hassad had asked him almost anything else. He understood Hassad's question as a challenge, albeit a gentle one: he had heard it said before that most Muslims understood their religion better than most Christians understood theirs. He recognized, too, the hunger of shepherds everywhere for a scrap of conversation rich enough to think over through many days of solitude.

"Let's walk toward your sheep, and toward the Pilgrim Way, and I will try to answer."

They set off, Greatheart at Thomas' heels. Thomas tried to think of Christianity in the simplest terms, simpler than the Ten Commandments, which came from Judaism; simpler even than the Nicene Creed.

"When Jesus was on earth," he said to Hassad, "he was preaching one day to a group of farmers and fishermen on a hill by a lake. He said that there were two commandments on which all the rest of religion depended."

"And what were they, these two commandments?"

"To love God with all your heart and soul and mind, and to love other people as yourself."

They walked in silence for a moment. Then Hassad put his hand to his forehead. "Hooooo-eeee! These two commandments are harder than all five of ours! To fast you can do even when you are angry. To say the prayers, yes, they will make you feel happier. I give alms whether I love the beggar or not, for my own good, to be holy. But always to have your heart turned the right way? Impossible! These are difficult commandments, sounding so gentle." He shook his head again, and said almost to himself, "No wonder Christians carry such anger. . . ."

These are not funeral bells," Fra Ramon told Fra Jaime of Sancti Spiritus. "Break the rhythm! Give it a little"—he lifted his robes and did a dance step, tapping his heels—"lift! It is a call of welcome."

Ringing the bells cheerfully, irregularly, hour after hour, wore Fra Jaime out, and he staggered gratefully to his cot.

Most of the pilgrims had taken off together toward Santiago. Only three were still at Sancti Spiritus: Fra Pietro, too feeble to walk; Martin; and Etienne. Each hid his worry over Elenor and Thomas.

Fra Pietro slept.

Martin, champion at the game of stone-putting, continued to hone his skills, resolutely not thinking.

Etienne grieved. He took from his pack the parchment scraps he had begged from Aimery, the bookseller, fingering them, wishing he had given them to Elenor as he had meant to do. *I'm a coward,* he thought. He had not given Elenor the scraps because he knew with absolute certainty that she would cry tears of joy. He knew how they would spring up in her gray eyes. He even knew, he thought, how she would feel. . . . And the affection between Elenor and Thomas was so fine, so frail. Etienne wanted to cup his hands around it the way Thomas cupped his around a tinder spark, to give it every chance.

He borrowed Martin's lute. He sat on a rock in the sun and wind, tried to ignore the bells, and sang softly to himself, trying out tunes, making up songs. Martin interrupted his practice to give advice:

"Make up some long story songs. We need long songs to make the road shorter.

"What about that story Fra Pietro told about the two pilgrims? Wouldna tha' make a good song?"

Later still he listened attentively. "That's verra nice. Now put in some kind of a refrain for people who canna remember the words. But first, one round of stones, to loosen up the fingers."

The Brothers of Sancti Spiritus rang the bells for as long as any pilgrim was lost in the pass. All night. All day.

Martin and Etienne disagreed about a point in their game. Nose to nose, both wild-eyed and ready to kill, they came to the same conclusion at the same time:

"We've got to get out of here!"

"The bells have driven us mad!"

"Holy Father Abbot," said Etienne, "we'll head back toward France and look for signs. We'll—"

"There'll be two of us; we'll be verra careful—"

"I have a song to try out."

The abbot rolled his eyes to heaven. "Stay on the path," he said.

Is it a song fit to walk to?" asked Etienne anxiously. Martin strode beside him, crooning harmony and making changes here and there; it took his mind off worrying about Elenor. Neither of them mentioned either her or Thomas, but they kept up the noise: anyone within half a mile would be sure to hear them. Rabbits ran for cover.

Pierre brought Elenor to the Way a few miles north of the hospice. There was no one in sight, but they could hear the bells ringing.

"I will leave you here, Nora. I must go back to my sheep, before they all get into mischief. And I do not wish for the priests to know I am here."

"Pierre," said Elenor, wishing there was something she could give him, and knowing that there wasn't.

"Yes, Nora." He took her chin in his hand and looked at her with his bright searching eyes.

"I will always remember you with joy," she said.

"And so will I remember you, Nora, with joy and some regrets." He kissed her forehead. "Now go!"

She did, running down the path, stopping only at the turning to look back and wave. She was crying.

Hassad was as reluctant as Pierre to go anywhere near the hospice. "This is not a good place for people of my religion," he explained to Thomas. "Many Christians expect us to be—" He jumped sideways, crouched, pretended to pull a cutlass from his belt, and snarled. Then he laughed. "I do not wish to hang. I have a great love of life, so I stay away from the trail of pilgrims." He gestured toward the mountainside. Then he pointed to Thomas and patted his chest. "Though some pilgrims I like very much."

"I understand," said Thomas. "I am sad to say good-bye already. Go with my thanks, and Hassad—"

"Yes?"

"*Salaam aleikoum*," Thomas said, putting his hands on his thighs and bowing.

"Wa aleikoum salaam," answered Hassad, bowing in the same way.

Thomas took off down the trail at a run, with Greatheart at his heels.

He ran longer and faster than Elenor and caught up to her before she had gone far. She heard the footsteps behind her and turned in alarm. She jumped in the air and ran toward him, almost tripping over Greatheart, who was mad with glee, and threw her arms around Thomas' neck. He lifted her off her feet and swung her around and kissed her tearful face, and then stopped and held her from him, gazing raptly. Greatheart seized the chance and jumped into her arms and began licking her face.

"I'm getting a good face washing today." She laughed shakily. "Oh, Thomas, I'm so sorry. I've made such trouble. But oh, Thomas, I'm so glad I got lost!"

"And found, too?"

"Oh, yes, and found, too."

Just then, Etienne and Martin came around the bend, singing lustily.

Fra Pietro was dying. His face had a pale and almost translucent radiance, the bones clear and prominent. He was, Elenor thought, like a person waiting for a ship to leave, though far less apprehensive than she had been at the sailing of the *Lady Elwyse*. Elenor held a cup of wine to his lips, but he drank very little. She wiped the rest off his chin gently and, dabbing the napkin on his pale lips, wondered if he had ever kissed anyone. She held his hand during the meal. Seeing that she could not get her hand free, Thomas cut her fish for her.

Fra Pietro had received last rites earlier in the afternoon. He made no effort to talk, but watched the Brothers and pilgrims, sometimes keenly, sometimes remotely, as his last energies came and went. Elenor was shaking with tiredness, and the evening stretched out for her like an endless dream. *Hurry up and die, Fra Pietro,* Elenor willed, *so I can sleep.* He held her hand. *Take your time, Fra Pietro. Take your blessed time,* she thought, contrite.

"Brother, we have put one of the stories you told us into a song. Would you like to hear it?" asked Etienne, and the old man smiled faintly. Etienne sang softly but very clearly. Martin joined him on harmonies, serious now, intent on making the best of the song. Shadows flickered on the whitewashed walls made pink by the firelight. The Brothers' faces, each so different, were serene. Greatheart thumped his tail gently. *Their voices are like a dance,* thought Elenor, too tired to blink back tears.

The story told of two pilgrims traveling together to Santiago. One pilgrim dies on the way, and the other continues, making the pilgrimage for them both. In the last verse of the song, the pilgrim is leaving the sanctuary at Santiago alone. He feels a hand on his shoulder and hears the voice of his companion. By the end of the song all of the Brothers were singing the refrain. They sang the last one over twice, a lullaby for Fra Pietro.

In the quiet after the song, his ragged breath came and went more and more slowly, each exhalation deep and complete, each new inhalation a restless interruption. Elenor thought of a dog settling to sleep, standing, turning, lying down again.

Fra Pietro gave Elenor's hand a squeeze, and died. The body on the stretcher was no more Fra Pietro than was the bench beside it.

Elenor swayed on her knees. Fra Jaime caught her before she hit the floor, and made her go to bed, where she fell into the deepest sleep of her life, with Greatheart warm and snoring at the crook of her knees.

25

Bonds

elcome, pilgrims! Welcome to Zubiri in the name of God and of his holy mother. Take a drink here. The water is sweet and there is plenty of it all the year round, thank God." An old lady dressed in black, her eyes sparkling in a sea of wrinkles, helped fill their gourds, as the pilgrims crowded around the fountain, drinking from cupped hands. A sow wallowed at their feet, adding her own cries of joy at the splashes of spilled water.

Going into the town out of the hot sun was like diving into a tunnel, or an animal's burrow. The houses were built so tightly together that they blocked out the light. Sheep, goats, and cattle trotted in the street as if down mountain gulches and were slapped and prodded into stables on the ground floor of people's houses.

In the dark, people called greeting and encouragement, and when they burst out into the sun

again, the pilgrims found a market-day welcome.

The church adjoined an old square. Roman columns held up the half-timbered porches of houses
and taverns. Merchants and farmers had their wares
spread out under the porches and around the
square. Beside a table piled with fresh-baked bread,
a child waved branches to keep off flies. Elenor
thought back to the day at Ramsay when they had
heard the men were coming home, so very long
ago, and wanted to pummel bread dough again;
she wanted to show off her muscles to Elise and
Helen.

Some men came into the square dragging a cart
loaded with pigskins of wine. Villagers took long
pulls, squirting the wine through the air and catching it in their mouths, and challenged the pilgrims
to do the same. Martin winked at Elenor when he
saw her admiring his skill. Thomas had wine on
his chin and on his shirt. He shrugged his shoulders
and held a wineskin out to her with a grin. No
other ladies were drinking straight from the skin,
she noticed, so she shook her head, but she felt
flooded with well-being.

She and Thomas slept separately now, by unspo-
ken agreement. Pierre had taught Elenor that men
could want her, and she herself could no longer
pretend that Thomas was Carla.

The sound of church bells brought people hurrying and hobbling down the streets from all sides; merchants left their wares unattended. After vespers, people stayed in the plaza, lingering in the summer dusk, and the music started. The pilgrims had been invited to bed down in the church or under the arcades of the plaza, but it seemed the townspeople had little intention of letting them sleep. A young man carrying a drum and a pipe danced in shuffling circles, playing a shrill repetitive tune with one hand, while keeping up a steady beat on the drum. Wherever he passed, everyone from toddlers to ancient grandpas raised their hands in the air, snapped their fingers, and stepped to the music. Elenor saw an old farmer showing Etienne the steps, cheering him on with yelps of encouragement, clapping him on the back and plying him with wine.

Well fed on bread and cheese, wine and grapes, Elenor asked a child where she could relieve herself, and was directed to a ditch that ran out under the wall at the low end of the village. Back in the plaza, she rolled herself in her cloak and, using her bag for a pillow, settled against one of the stone columns. She watched the colorful blur of festivities through half-closed eyes and was soon asleep.

Sometime in the night Elenor had a dream of bugs singing in harmony. She woke to the voices of old, old ladies. Opening her eyes, she saw seven crones moving through the plaza to the light of a lantern that one of them held aloft. Another held a human skull, turning its grin one way and another like royalty greeting a crowd. Merrily they called out in singsong voices, "Pray for the souls in purgatory! Wake up, you sleepers, and say one little prayer for your brothers and sisters in purgatory, waiting for the glory of God. Just one little prayer, and then sleep well." Among them, Elenor recognized the old woman who had welcomed them at the fountain.

Lauds was already ringing when she woke. Elenor sat up in the pale light, chewing a stick to clean her teeth, dreading the trip to the ditch. When she came back, she combed her hair. It took a long time to get it free of snarls, and her arm ached. Her hair was almost to her waist now, and it was a relief to get it plaited and looped up out of the way.

She let her eyes rest on Thomas. He twitched and pulled his blanket closer in his sleep. His head rested on the hard stone of the square. An old man hobbled from group to group of sleeping pilgrims, shaking them awake. Elenor watched him grab Thomas' foot. Thomas gave a kick that sent the old man sprawling, then instantly staggered to his feet, apologizing and helping the man up.

"So sorry, brother—didn't mean to hurt you—took me by surprise. Here, have you breakfasted?"

Poor Thomas.

The man's name was Gregoire. He had fallen sick here in Zubiri years ago on his way to Santiago.

"I stayed at the church for many nights, and every day people brought me their good bread and their wine, their prayers, too, and a little girl came and sang to me, so that I hoped to die here and never leave, knowing the women would pray for my soul along with the others."

"But you got well," Elenor prompted.

"Yes, *hija,* I got well, but then I realized that I didn't need to keep traveling, for if the people of Zubiri could forgive my wickedness, then surely God, who is greater in kindness, had forgiven me long since."

Chewing yesterday's bread and sipping water from their gourds, Thomas and Elenor thought over what Gregoire said.

Thomas spoke. "Tell me, brother, how do you think that this undertaking of a pilgrimage helps us to win forgiveness?"

Gregoire took his time in answering.

"Horses," he said flatly at last, startling Elenor. "Battle horses. You have to train them, right?"

Thomas nodded.

"You put them through trials. You make them tough. The world, the temptations and hard times and sorrows toughen us, readying us for heaven. That's how." He nodded emphatically.

Later, when they had said good-bye to Gregoire and to Zubiri, and the path again became wide enough so that they could walk side by side, Elenor asked Thomas what he thought of the old man's answer.

"I think that for Gregoire his pilgrimage worked as expiation." Thomas hesitated. "The baker told me that, years ago, Gregoire flew into a jealous rage and murdered his whole family. He was banished from his village and wore a sign saying I AM A MURDERER, until he settled in Zubiri."

"Like Cain," said Elenor, and shivered. "But what if you like being on pilgrimage? How can it be a trial? I mean, what if you would rather be on pilgrimage than doing anything else? How would it toughen your soul?"

"You can be happy and tough both, don't you think?" said Thomas. "A battle horse enjoys his training."

"But I haven't done anything hard yet."

Thomas thought about her giving away Mab, carrying Jean-Paul, holding Fra Pietro's hand, but he didn't contradict her, for surely she would know better than he what was hard for her and what wasn't. Instead he asked, "Do you like being on this pilgrimage, and in my company?"

He sounded so pleased with himself, as if he had invented the whole idea of pilgrimage, that some of Elenor's misgivings came back. But she could still say, "Yes, Thomas of Thornham-Ramsay, except for the bugs and the latrine ditches and a few of the maudlin songs, I like it very much indeed." They walked on companionably in silence until Thomas spoke again.

"Then what, for you, would be a trial of fire?"

Without thinking she answered, "Boredom. To be the lady on the tapestry and spend my life waiting. Also, to bear children."

"Oh," said Thomas.

Elenor was embarrassed.

"But maybe that wouldn't be so bad, either, once I, ah, put my mind to it," she mumbled.

At Puente la Reina a major road joined theirs, bringing in pilgrims from the south of France, Italy, Romania, even Greece. Elenor suddenly felt shy and tired. She was ashamed of her timidity. It didn't help that some of these new pilgrims were girls almost as young as she was, big Italian girls who traveled together confidently, with no men, and laughed and joked together, their voices like music, like bubbly water. Elenor saw one of them watching Thomas, catching his eye and giving him a broad smile, only to be teased and scolded by her companions. They didn't notice Elenor.

A third road led due south to Saragossa. This was the road that Etienne must take to get to Toledo. They had traveled together for so long that it seemed impossible to Elenor that they would not be seeing Etienne anymore, hearing his voice in the night and his songs along the road. She, Thomas, and Etienne stood at the crossroad shrine, not wanting to say good-bye.

"Come with us to Compostela," Thomas urged him.

"Remember my quest, Thomas? To learn about Islam and the world of the Arabs? Maybe, Thomas, our quests are the same. *You* come with me."

Elenor could tell that Thomas longed to do just that. They had talked over what each had learned from Hassad, and Elenor was surprised to find that Thomas was familiar with the Koran. Etienne had shown them both what he knew of Arabic writing, and the three of them had practiced flourishing Arabic letters in the dust when no other pilgrims were around.

Elenor was beginning to see that Thomas had a

lively, curious, and patient mind. She wished, for his sake, that he could go to Toledo, or to some great center of learning. Maybe in England . . .

"Maybe your travels will bring you to England someday," Thomas was saying to Etienne, but none of them could really picture such a faraway future.

"Thank you for the stories and the songs," said Elenor. "I have them here." She pointed to her head. "I'll write them down when I get home."

"Under your hat, are they?" said Etienne, putting his hand on her head in a gesture that was half caress, half blessing. "I've been wondering what was under that hat. Oh!" he added nonchalantly, fishing parchment scraps from his satchel. "These are to write them down on, or for pictures." Tears sprang to Elenor's eyes.

With hugs all around, they parted company. When Etienne was very small in the distance, he turned, and they waved energetically at each other from one end to the other of the dusty road.

Thomas and Elenor had fallen behind the main body of pilgrims, and they were in no hurry to catch up. The road was so dry it would take a long time for the dust to settle. They walked off the path a ways. Conversation seemed a great effort.

"I need to find a place to wash clothes," said Elenor, to break the silence.

"Fleas?" asked Thomas.

Elenor nodded. "Big Zubiri fleas, and maybe lice."

They followed a sheep path that started within sight of the dusty road. Farther on, the flatness of the land gave way to hills, and the path meandered into a pine woods. The trees shaded them; the needles cushioned their footsteps; the heat of the day opened the pinecones so that the air was mellow with the smell of rosin. They walked as in a dream, quietly, and the path became indiscernible in the play of light and shadow, the soft browns and greens and coppers. Elenor had a tremendous desire to lie down in the soft pine needles. She saw little sandy burrows under the roots where rabbits surely nestled. She followed Thomas, heedless as a sleepwalker.

"Can we take a rest?" she finally asked, just as she was stumbling to her knees.

"Aye," said Thomas, "I think we must, for how else can we find out where we are now? This is a strange wood with no moss on the trees." He squatted down and, clearing away pine needles, drew a big circle on the ground. "If we stay still for an hour or so, perhaps we'll see how the sun moves, and then we can follow it to the southwest and meet the Way." He took a little stick, put it upright in the ground, and drew a line where its shadow ran. "And now we wait," he said contentedly. But

Elenor was already nestled in a spot of sun, her pack under her head, fast asleep.

He was there when she woke up; she knew it without seeing him. His being there added warmth to a day already hot and dancing with the smell of pine sap and the hum of little forest insects. She rolled over and found him watching her, his eyes dark and serious. She longed to roll over twice more and bury herself in his warmth and forget about being a pilgrim. Instead, she sat up and started picking pine needles out of her hair.

"Let me," said Thomas. She was wondrously surprised to see that his hands were shaking.

It was well past noon when they found the Way again. The road was empty, save for a solitary tinker who struck up conversation with Thomas. Elenor hurried on ahead. She heard the faint sound of water, could feel a freshness in the air, and soon came to a newly built stone bridge arching over a small river.

The water tumbled over rocks, a good sign: fast-running water was usually clean and drinkable. But Elenor's heart sank: there were already some women in the river doing their wash, and among them she recognized several Italian girls and Melinda. She fought off an impulse to hurry on. She shouldered up her bundle and climbed down the embankment.

The women paused for a minute in their talking and looked at her with friendly curiosity. She nodded a greeting, dumped her bundle on the bank, and threw her heavy cape toward the water. A clamor went up from the girls. They clustered around her, holding the cape up, feeling the wool, shaking their heads.

In the babble of voices Elenor recognized three words: *mal,* which meant "bad," *lavare,* which could only mean "wash," and *lana,* which had to be "wool." They were worried that she would ruin her cloak by washing it. She forgot her shyness in the involved ritual of talking in signs and mixed languages. She put her hand on one girl's shoulder to get her attention.

"Look, *regarde, mira.*" She showed her where the cape had become infested, probably from sleeping against the column in Zubiri. She showed how big the cape was on her, trying to show that it could use a little shrinking. There were shruggings of shoulders and shakings of heads, but finally one girl brought over a pot of soft soap and shouted to the others. Elenor heard *ajuda,* the Latin word for "help," and *inglesa,* "English girl."

The others flocked around and plunged into

helping Elenor do what they had all advised her not to do. They soaked the heavy wool and rubbed the soft soap through it. Then they trampled it underfoot on the clean gravel bottom of the river, stomping out soap and dirt and vermin together. Clouds of black dirt and dye swirled downstream. One girl suddenly shrieked, shaking a blackened foot in the air, and they all began inspecting their bare feet. Three girls put their arms on one another's shoulders and did a line dance, shaking first one foot, then the other.

"*E come se chiama la piccola inglesa?*" asked one. Elenor was catching on to the language. They were asking her name.

"Nora," she said, pointing at herself, and "*Tu?*" touching the girl nearest her.

"Anna," the girl answered.

"*Io* Bea!" said the biggest, most beautiful and outspoken of the girls, the one who had been trying to get Thomas' attention, with such a flourish that the others laughed and cheered.

They were so splashed they gave up trying to keep dry. Bea tucked her skirts in her belt and waded in up to her thighs, and the others followed. Washing all the clothes was a long job, standing in the icy water, but at last Elenor and the others hauled the heavy cape up onto a grassy part of the bank, wrung it out, and spread it in the afternoon sun. Elenor's feet were numb and her back ached. She sank contentedly to the ground watching the others spread their clothes on rosemary bushes.

And when they had finished and stretched out beside her, Thomas appeared, carrying his cloak to the washing. He was met with a roar from the Italian girls, a roar of greeting, protest, and exasperation.

Wouldn't it be fine," said Thomas after supper, as they lay around the campfire ready for sleep, "wouldn't it be sensible if we could just forget who is supposed to do what?"

"Shall we have a debate about it?" asked Elenor, with a yawn.

"A disputation . . ."

"Aye," said Martin, who had turned up again after a week in someone's wine cellar, "aren't we doing just that? Look at Nora. Long ago, she was an English lady; now she sets snares, fishes, cooks—"

"Hardly, Martin," muttered Elenor, who had burned the fish for supper.

"And she can read and write like an abbot."

Elenor, embarrassed, tried to change the tide of the conversation. "There's Thomas, who washed his own cloak this afternoon, with a little help from the Italian *brigata*—"

"No!" broke in Martin, clasping his hands over his heart. "Not my Italians!"

"While our wandering poet looked for the meaning of life in a skin of Rioja wine," continued Elenor. "Why get stuck with being just one person? Thomas, are you thinking of taking up the priesthood?"

Her question, asked flippantly, hung in the air a moment, and a sudden sadness hit Elenor in the pit of the stomach. Did she care what he answered? Anyway, she had broken the mood of joking without meaning to.

"Well," Thomas said at last, "I think I would like to study with a wise person like Bernard of Chartres, or Abelard, and surely there are some such great scholars teaching now." He stared into the fire a little wistfully; then he smiled. "I don't think, though, that I'd like to be a priest."

"Why not?" asked Elenor.

"I wouldn't like being celibate, for one thing," said Thomas, smiling but not looking at her as he rolled over and turned his back on his companions.

"Ha!" Martin snorted. "And ye think the priests are?"

26

The Brigata

Elenor was beginning to hate her heavy cape. She still used it to sleep on, to keep her off the ground, but all day every day now she carried it on her back, rolled as tightly as she could get it. The sun poured down on the high plateaus of northern Spain like honey; she swam in it step after step and felt as if she would never be cold again. Underfoot, dry desert flowers opened and blossomed and were crushed to powder. The air was full of the drone of insects.

"Did you know that Saint Francis used to stop and pick little bugs off the road and set them on the side so they wouldn't get trampled?" asked Anna, one of the Italian girls.

"It's a wonder he ever made it to Compostela, then," replied Elenor shortly. With a whispery crunch, herbs powdered underfoot, releasing a tangy smell. Tiny bees swarmed around the herbs and wildflowers, oblivious to the passing humans.

One landed on Melinda's skirt, and she shook it off gently.

"At home we believe that bees are the souls of babies who are waiting to be born. And so we are very careful."

"That's depressing," said Elenor, looking at the millions of bees around her.

"Why?" asked Bea, who was striding steadily on her other side. "Don't you want to have many babies, you and Thomas?" The Italian girls all laughed.

"Bea is jealous," teased Gisella, and Bea blushed, but she put an arm around Elenor's shoulders.

"Look at them all." She smiled. "Just waiting."

Elenor swallowed. She was very thirsty. "Maybe just one," she said hoarsely. "But you can never have just one, can you?"

"Well," said Bea, "maybe and maybe not." What a child this English girl was! Didn't she know anything? "But if you're lucky and want to, you can take a good long rest between each of them."

"Can you really? And for how long?" Elenor had never known anyone whom she had thought to ask these questions.

"Oh, two years, anyway. You just keep nursing the first one, and like as not, you won't get another until you stop."

Elenor laughed. She knew that about milk cows. Why hadn't she guessed it would be true of women, too? What foolishness it seemed that ladies put their babies out to nurse with wet nurses and then died of too many births too close together! Suddenly the day seemed very beautiful.

"Start a song, Bea."

Bea threw back her head and called out to the blue sky, *"Utreeeeeiiiiaaaa!"* which was picked up by Elenor and Melinda and Gisella and pilgrims all up and down the Way. But they were all too thirsty for the singing to last long.

"Tell us a story, Bea," said Gisella.

"*Oc.* Here's one I heard in Puente. It's about how they got their school for children there."

"Tell it."

"Once upon a time, actually about fifty years ago, the town of Puente la Reina in the kingdom of Navarre had a very greedy mayor. He was one of those fellows who hates terribly to part with his money, and yet he loved fine clothes, fine tapestries, and, above all, fine food.

"As this mayor was passing through the market one day, checking the scales of the merchants and keeping everyone honest, he spied in a fish stall a most beautiful mackerel, fresh and shiny silver, with an eye so clear it seemed to have just jumped out of the ocean.

" 'Merchant!' said the mayor. 'What do you want for that fish?'

" 'Ah! Lord Mayor, that is the best of fish, and for it I am asking one gold peso.'

" 'A gold peso! For a simple fish! You must be mad, man!'

"The merchant did not answer, but simply shrugged his shoulders and bowed in a humble way. The mayor strode away in a huff, and went home, where he sat on an embroidered chair and thought about how good that fish would have tasted. At last he was unable to bear the temptation. He called for his servant, and once again he headed for the market. When he got to the fish stall, the beautiful fish was gone! The merchant must have put it in the shade somewhere.

" 'Ahem! Merchant! I have decided to buy the fish. The large one that was right here. Where is it now?'

" 'Ah, Lord Mayor, I am sorry to tell you that that fish has been sold.'

" 'Sold! At the price you told me?'

"The merchant nodded.

" 'Who in this town can possibly have bought a fish for that price? Why, a person could get a pair of good shoes for a gold peso!' The mayor was outraged to think that anyone had more money to spend than he did, and he was even more outraged when he thought of someone else eating that delicious fish.

" 'I believe that may be just what happened, sir,' said the merchant. 'The person who bought the fish was a poor cobbler, but he told me he had just been paid the peso for a pair of boots.'

" 'Is he nearby?' asked the mayor. 'I would like to speak with the man.'

" 'Yes, right over there.'

"So the mayor strode up to the little cobbler, who stood holding his young son by the hand, a large fish-shaped parcel under his arm.

" 'You, fellow. Did you just buy the large mackerel that was for sale over there?'

" 'Yes, sir. I did,' said the cobbler, a smile spreading over his face.

" 'And how could you afford to spend money so irresponsibly?'

"The cobbler seemed at a loss for a reply, but after thinking a moment, he said, 'Lord Mayor, this is a truly exceptional fish, and with it my family and I will have a truly exceptional meal, which we can remember on days when we are hungry.'

" 'But have you no savings?' asked the mayor. 'What will happen to you if you fall sick?'

"The cobbler scratched his head. 'If I am sick, some kind soul will help me. There is, I think, a charity hospital in this town.'

"When he heard this, the mayor was even more incensed, for in his will, which he had drawn up before a magistrate, he had left all his wealth to the charity hospital. It had seemed a good way to assure himself a place in heaven. Now he thought about how this cobbler would enjoy fish while he, the mayor, who had accumulated so much wealth, would dine on something ordinary. He went home and called the magistrate.

" 'I want to change my will,' he said. 'I will not leave anything at all to the charity hospital. Instead, I will leave all my wealth to build a school for the children of Puente, that they may grow up to be wise. It will be open to all children except the children of cobblers, who have enough good fortune already.'

"And as far as I know," said Bea, "that is the true story of how Puente got its school."

"And children of cobblers still can't go?"

"That's what I was told," said Bea.

"Did you ever go to school, Nora?" asked Gisella. "You can read, can't you?"

Elenor told her about Father Gregory's tutoring. "And what about you?"

The Italian girls all looked at each other and laughed.

"We all go to school together," began Gisella.

"*Went* to school, Gisella. It's over now, don't you remember?"

"When we were all working as shepherdesses in

Tuscany, we used to meet for lunch in the shade of some willow trees near the church. We ate and rested and talked—"

"And pretended we were queens."

"And climbed the trees."

"When I was six and Bea was ten, she fed me mud pies!"

"And Gisella ate them, *poverina,*" teased Bea.

"You've all known each other that long?" Elenor asked.

"Oh, yes. We are a *brigata*. We stick together."

"And what about the school?"

"There was a wonderful old priest at the church—"

"A saint!"

"Fra Giacomo. He came out one day and said—"

"He said, 'As long as you girls are here every day, we should have a little school.' And he broke off sticks from the tree and started teaching us our letters."

Bea stopped and traced in the dirt, while the other girls chanted slowly, "A-V-E M-A-R-I-A!"

"If it hadn't been for Fra Giacomo, our fathers would never have let us do this pilgrimage; mine wouldn't have, anyway," said Anna.

"After we told him what we wanted to do, he went to each house and talked so long to our parents, saying how brave we are, and religious, and sensible . . ." They all laughed, and Bea made a halo with her hands over Gisella's head. "And how we will work so much harder and better when we come home again."

"I won't complain about walking from Petrella to Cascalenda, that's for sure."

Thomas watched Nora, Melinda, and the Italian girls from below as they came down a hill— six black figures against the landscape of endless red earth hills. They were all practicing carrying their bundles on their heads, and their laughter floated down to him. From this distance they looked very tall, as if the bundles were extensions of their heads. It was evening. Shadows stretched long, the sky was deep blue, the hills striped rust and gold, deep rich colors. A flock of blackbirds rose suddenly from a shadowed dip into the copper sun.

27

Calvary

E lenor grabbed at a small tree to pull herself up a steep stretch. It occurred to her that those who had first worn and then paved the Pilgrim Way didn't much care about getting to Santiago. Their aim was to get close to God. They built shrines on the tops of mountains. The harder the mountain was to climb, the better.

Santa Lucia was a pilgrimage church built where nothing grew but stunted pines, up where it was windy and cold even in August. A hundred and thirty stone steps were carved into the highest peak, on its steepest side. To climb these steps on their knees, saying an Ave Maria on each step, and a Paternoster every ten, one for each Station of the Cross, was called by the pilgrims a Calvary. It was designed to make the pilgrim suffer the way Jesus suffered on his way to being crucified.

Thomas and Elenor stopped to rest on the mountainside across the valley from Santa Lucia.

"Melinda is doing the Calvary tomorrow," said Elenor.

"Our martyr Melinda. She'll faint halfway up."

"Melinda says she wants to do the Calvary as a pledge."

"A pledge of what?"

"Toward honesty, I think; not to tell fortunes or fake visions anymore."

"Why choose such a dramatic way of making a pledge? I don't see how climbing those steps on your knees is any different from scourging yourself with a flail. It's the kind of thing Friar Paul might tell somebody to do." Thomas peeled some pine sap from a tree, rolling it between his fingers. "Doesn't it seem perverse to you, Nora, to act as if pain were holy, and pleasure a sin?"

Elenor thought suddenly of the pine woods, the strong pull of pleasure that seemed to have no wrong in it except that it was forbidden. She thought of Pierre, of his honest, questioning face, eyebrows raised.

"I don't know," she said. And she didn't. Back at Ramsay, she had always thought that Friar Paul was perverse in his love of pain, but she wondered lately if she had misunderstood him or been too quick to dismiss his every sermon because of his ugly body and his squeaky voice.

"Melinda says that voluntary submission to pain is a virtue, in imitation of Christ."

"Maybe," said Thomas. "But Christ didn't ask to be crucified, did he? It was the outcome of his work. He dreaded it. He prayed to be spared."

Elenor nodded, agreeing, while the words she meant to say next stuck in her throat.

"Thomas, we—I—am doing the Calvary with Melinda. All of the *brigata*, too. Because we are her friends."

Thomas threw the sticky rosin away. His mouth tightened and he looked out over the valley.

Elenor felt desolate. Before he had come back to England, she had never expected that she and Thomas of Thornham would agree on anything; in the last few months the bond between them had become her greatest joy. Now that she was deliberately doing something he did not agree with, she felt as if she were breaking a trust.

"I let Melinda know when I thought she was being stupid; I should let her know when I think she's doing right," she managed to say, but her heart wasn't in it.

"Couldn't you just tell her?" tried Thomas.

Elenor shook her head. Afraid she would lose her resolve, she got up and left to find the *brigata*.

Thomas picked up a rock and threw it hard

against a tree. Was Elenor going to become a Doomsdayer and join Friar Paul's keeners at Ramsay? He would hate that. He had thought that he and Nora agreed that self-inflicted pain was perverse. He had thought that she shared his distrust of overpious ladies who spent their time crying on their knees. He thought about her pigheadedness and the prospect of marriage.

Elenor slept with the *brigata* that night.

Thomas and Martin shared a jug of wine and then rolled up in their cloaks under the stars. The cold wind blew along the ground, smelling of mountain sage. Thomas fell into a deep and forlorn dream: he was in a large, luminous gray room. Before him he could see the black squared shoulders of a woman kneeling, facing away from him. Her face was hidden, but he could see the white shaft of her bent neck, the black mass of her bound hair. He could hear the repetitious words of prayer. He was unable to speak, but all of his being longed for the woman to turn toward him. The words of the prayers fell on him in gray pebbles, covering him, weighing him down, constricting his chest like swaddling bands. The woman never turned.

Elenor, Bea, Gisella, Anna, Irena, and Melinda bought rags from the children who hawked them at the bottom of the Calvary, and tied them around their knees. "Else we'll not get to the top, much less to Santiago," said Irena.

"God doesn't mind, or he'd strike down these little varmints for selling the rags," reasoned Bea.

Together they began the climb, Bea and Melinda leading off with the first half of the Ave Maria, the others coming in on *"Sancta Maria, mater dei,"* and continuing through to "Amen," at which point they moved to the next step and Bea and Melinda began again. Elenor took pleasure in the sound of their voices as the familiar words flowed and jumbled together. Bea speeded things up by beginning her *"Ave"* just before Elenor said "Amen," and bit by bit, the two groups overlapped more and more, so that the prayers flowed faster and faster and there was no time to rest on a step before shifting onto one knee to climb to the next. Moving up the steps was very awkward: the steps were high.

Every ten steps there was a tiny side chapel, a place where the ground leveled out enough for them to crawl off the steps and rest. In the first of these chapels they found a comforting statue of San Roque, the patron saint of cuts and bruises, showing his scraped knees.

"Nice knees, Roque," said Bea.

"I'm going to turn into a goose before this is over," muttered Anna.

The second decena was twice as hard as the first, and when the girls reached the chapel of San Blas, patron of sore throats, they rolled over and stretched their legs and cried with relief.

By the third chapel they were leaning on each other for support, dragging one another up by the elbows.

By the fifth chapel, Elenor's knees were raw, and sharp pains shot through her hip joints. Her mind wandered and she half dreamed she had been turned into a dwarf for ingratitude.

From the sixth chapel, dedicated to Our Lady of Sorrows, they could look back over the valleys. The sun was setting and mist rose from a river below. But it made Elenor dizzy to look down, and miserable to look up. Waves of nausea swept over her. They were only halfway. She was determined not to faint.

On and on it went. The rags bit into her knees, and then one came untied, so that she left a splotch of blood on each step. She didn't notice. She was intent on gathering up her pain and offering it as a prayer. All of her concentration was on dragging herself up one more step, and one more after that. The flow of prayers slowed, as each step became a struggle between body and spirit.

It was dark before they reached the top. Candles burned in the church, constantly relit as they blew out in the drafts. The air was acrid with smoke, and Elenor saw only a blaze of light, because her eyes were swimming. It was over; they had all made it; and Elenor collapsed on the hard rock of the church threshold.

A Sister from the hostel attached to the church of Santa Lucia had just revived her when Thomas found them. He picked her up as she came to, and when she protested, he couldn't think of anything to say, but rocked her gently. He carried her to the hostel and made his way through the crowd to a place near the fire, because she was shaking. When a Sister came by with a bowl of water for washing the knees of the penitents, he took it from her and very gently washed the blood off Elenor's knees. There were no words spoken between them.

The rule is, water and bread for one day for each pilgrim, and then he has to move along, unless he's sick, like your friend here. She's got to stay a few days, until her fever's gone, God bless her, but we can't be feeding the lot of you while you wait for her to get well."

The hallway outside the tiny cell where Elenor lay shivering and sweating was crowded; the four Italian girls were there, and Thomas and Martin, and Melinda, who had brought her well-worn Saint Christopher medal for Elenor. Sister Antonia tried to quiet them down, and at last it was decided that the *brigata* would go on, Melinda with them. Thomas and Martin would be allowed to wait for Elenor and bring her along as soon as she could travel, provided they put a new roof on the barn for the Sisters.

"We'll hurry, and you travel as slowly as you can. We'll catch up with you in a few days," Martin told them. Each of the girls hugged Martin and Thomas good-bye, while Sister Antonia looked on impatiently. Martin was taking advantage of the confusion to start on a second round of hugs when the Sister finally pushed them all outside.

Thomas was glad and sorry to see them go. It touched him to see them limping down the steep mountainside, joking and supporting one another so much like wounded men after a battle.

He liked the *brigata,* especially Bea. He loved the way she looked and the way she moved, and he thought of her often, though he tried not to. As his affection for Nora was growing, so was his appreciation of all other women. It was troublesome.

Way at the bottom of the steep path, Bea turned to wave.

What an onion! Elenor held it between her hands; it filled them both, smooth and brown. Her throat ached; her eyes watered; she could hardly breathe. Outside the nuns' hostel, the wind howled, banging the wooden door, moaning down the chimney, scattering ashes and coals. Elenor had been huddled by the fire all morning, her only job to sweep the coals back into place with a hearth broom. Thomas was squatting by the fire now, squirting water from a pigskin into the kettle. His voice mingled with the sounds of the wind.

"One of these old Sisters used to be a curing woman. *La Curandera,* they call her. Back home, I don't know ... They took me to her cell."

"Is she—a witch?" Elenor croaked.

Thomas turned to see if he could tease her, but she looked so small and scared he decided against it.

"She's not a witch, or if she is, she's the helping kind. A little magic mixed with the prayers can't hurt. It's just that she's got a face like a mandrake root. And the only way she was going to come out to see you was if I carried her in a sack. I told her how you were shaking, your head on fire, your knees big as pig bladders ... no offense. 'Go straightaway to the kitchens,' she told me. 'Yes, ma'am!' I said. 'And get the biggest onion they've got. Make her eat the whole thing raw, and wash it down with hot wine. When she's sweating like a horse, call one of the Sisters to come and bring some holy water and wash off the sweat. That'll get rid of the fever and shakes,' she said, 'sure as Judgment Day.' " Thomas put his thumb in the kettle to test the water. "Sister Antonia thinks the knees are almost healed. It's just the fever we have to cure. There. Tell her there's hot water here when she comes in."

Stop being so busy, thought Elenor. *Just rock me.* "Thanks for the onion," she whispered as he went out the door.

Sister Antonia came in as Thomas went out, carrying holy water and a white cloth. Elenor obediently took her first chomp.

Later, after she had cried more tears than she thought she had in her, the fever broke and she slept like a baby, dreaming gentle dreams of ponies and flowers. Two days later fierce Sister Antonia told her to get on the road, and she did, though Thomas carried her bundle after they were out of the Sister's sight.

28

Slowing

At Los Condes they came to a shallow but fast-running river. A burly man sat in a heavy, painted rowboat, waiting to ferry the pilgrims across. He told Elenor that he had been carrying pilgrims over the river for thirty years.

"Have you ever been to Santiago?" she asked him.

The man shook his head. "I don't feel the need to travel yet," he said. "Maybe one day, when I've finished looking at the river."

Elenor watched the breeze ruffle the water, the delicate willow leaves trailing from the banks in green lacy curtains, and heard the plop of frogs and fish. The stones along the bank were golden in the sun, cool and brown in the water. Sheep grazed right up to the edge of the river, their bells clinking gently, their grunts conversational as they tore softly at the grass. Behind them rose the mellow stone wall of the convent of Santa Clara, broken by a welcoming arched portal decorated with zigzags of stone, rows of stone baubles, as sure and exuberant as a child's drawing. The gates stood open, and a ewe looked out, her head raised, sun shining on her wool so that she glowed. Elenor smiled at the boatman. "I don't think you will ever run out of things to see on the river."

He laughed. "Neither do I, little girl. So you must say a prayer for me in Santiago."

"And you must say one for me here. It is very good to be in one place."

She thought how glad she would be to be home, to see one particular lamb grow into a sheep, to see one particular tree flower and leaf out and make fruit and wither and bloom again.

On the arched ceiling of the church in León, Elenor saw paintings so beautiful she lay awake thinking of them all night, of the ochers and earth reds, the soft blues, the expressive sheep and sad-eyed shepherds.

The Way was crowded now, the pilgrimage like a river gathering strength. Too much to see, too much to hear. Too many stories and reasons and wishes. It made Elenor want to stop.

"Could we leave the Way?" she asked Thomas. "Could we take a side path? Or better yet, no path?"

"Why?" asked Thomas. But he was tired of having dust in his teeth.

"I want to slow down." She wasn't ready to get to Santiago.

Thomas thought about it. "After Ponferrada, the Way branches. We could take whichever branch seems less traveled."

So she walked patiently, listening to the stories, the songs, hoping to find the *brigata*. Greatheart walked at her heels, his tongue hanging out.

At Ponferrada, the pilgrims were lodged against the lower walls of a castle high above a river that snaked and shivered on its shale bed. The hostel and church were roofed in slate set in patterns like the scales of a dragon, gleaming in the rain. Only the intense greenness relieved the austerity of the place, and brilliant pink wild vines. Elenor pulled one of these to tickle the nose of a black kitten, until Greatheart chased it away. Could such a pink ever be transmitted to paper? Light but intense. *Some berry must have a juice like that,* she thought, scratching Greatheart behind the ears.

The Way forked. The main road led on to Santiago through a long valley. Another path went up over the hills, along the ridges, reaching Santiago in fewer miles over higher mountains. The lower road was the more frequented, and was well served by hostels. Elenor, Thomas, and Martin decided to take the high road.

Climbing ever higher, they could see the pilgrims on the pass road below, like ants, and they could hear snatches of song and the droning high notes of a Galician bagpipe.

> *"Herru Sanctiagu*
> *Got Sanctiagu*
> *E ultreia, e sus eia*
> *Deus, adjuva nos."*

The hills rose in gentle, powerful waves. Sometimes the path ran along the ridge of the mountain, with green fields falling away steeply, down, down to patches of forest where charcoal burners' fires smoked, down to the valley where sheep looked like tiny aphids, down to rushing streams.

The cool gray air made Elenor feel strong. She wrapped her cloak around her, flinging one end up over her shoulder so that no wind could get in. Her staff still felt heavy, but it was useful, too, for in places the path gave out altogether and she had to scramble over rocks and up ledges. She was glad to have it crossing streams as well, something to lean on when a rock tipped suddenly underfoot. Greatheart bounced at her heels. When she jumped from one rock to the next, he jumped, too, never seeming to realize there might not be room for both of them.

Greatheart was always hungry. One day of green fields and gray rocks and gray windy sky, he came bursting out of the heather with a rabbit in his mouth. Martin and Thomas gave him such applause that he dropped the rabbit, ran to Elenor, and rolled over backward, squirming with embarrassment and pleasure. Elenor skinned the rabbit a little sadly while Thomas built a fire, scraping and washing the skin, leaving it complete with ears, planning vaguely to make something soft for someone.

Ninety days to Santiago, Father Gregory had said. Elenor had lost count of the days they had been on the road: in León, Thomas had figured one hundred. Sometimes the gusts of wind coming in from the west carried the taste of the sea. Elenor did not look for an end to the pilgrimage. She had no wish to arrive in Santiago. Each day was complete, and the chores of survival absorbed her completely: gathering firewood, hunting or trapping, cooking, finding water, walking westward.

And looking. Martin found her lying on her back, one eye closed and the other staring into the throat of a blue morning-glory blossom.

"You're a lazy lass, you are. And do you think we'll be home before the snow flies, at this pace?"

"I'm not lazy," stated Elenor without moving, "nor do I care if I never get home." And she realized that this was almost true.

Martin went back to pitching trees, "tossing the cawber," he called it, with Thomas. It was something Scots did for fun, and Thomas was good at it. With his wild yells he reminded Elenor of his fourteen-year-old self.

Every once in a while, one of them remembered a new song, and they seized on it and sang it over and over until they were sick of it but couldn't get it out of their heads. They carried on the rambling conversations of people who have gotten to know each other very well. Thomas and especially Elenor pumped Martin to tell them about all the places he had been, and Martin stretched the truth in his enthusiasm to amaze and entertain them.

"Martin," said Thomas as they settled around the fire to sleep, "tells me that he has traveled almost to the Garden of Eden."

Elenor was skeptical. "Does it still exist somewhere? Is it in this world?"

"He talked to someone who was there. Martin! Wake up! Tell Nora your story."

Martin rolled over to face her across the fire.

"He was a verra old man I met on the road in Persia. He asked if I could help him, and I asked where it was he wanted to go. And he said to the garden, the Garden of Eden. I thought he was joking, and I said, 'Father, you would have to go back in time for that, back to the time before Adam sinned, and none of us can do that.' But he said, 'No, no, my son, don't believe that, for I have been to the Garden, and have seen it with my own eyes. . . .' And he took my arm, and as we walked, he said, 'The trees and plants there are of surpassing color and have a thousand scents that never fade, and they heal a person of any ill. The little birds sing in harmony, and the rustling of the leaves and the rippling of the streams make music. The rocks are jeweled, and the sands brighter than silver, and the breeze is gentle and health-giving, so that no one can ever be sick there.' "

Martin lay flat on his back, watching the sparks fly up to join the stars. Thomas looked across the fire at Nora.

"Shall we go there?" he asked. His face no longer looked ugly to her. *So that's what we're trying to do,* thought Elenor. *Go back to the Garden. . . .*

"When I asked the old man which way the Garden might be," continued Martin in his sleepy voice, "he turned his face up to the sun, and I could see that he was blind. 'Toward the heat,' he said. 'Always go toward the heat. The Garden is surrounded by a wall of fire as tall as from here to the moon.' "

Thomas turned on his back, pulled his rolled-up cloak under his neck, and stared up at the stars.

"No wonder he was lost, poor man, following the sun from east to west, day after day." Martin seemed to have dozed off. Elenor wished she could cross the fire.

Early the next morning, Martin spotted a tiny cross on the crest of one of the waves of hills that rose around them.

"If I'm not far wrong," he said, "that cross marks the pass at Cebrera. From there I hear tell that on a clear day you can see the spires of Santiago."

"And if you *are* far wrong ..." said Elenor, laughing, exhilarated and awed by their human smallness in this hugeness of mountains.

All day, they made their way toward the cross, without seeming to get any nearer. Clouds clung to trees below them. Hawks and sea gulls circled between them and the misty valley bottoms. By midday, only a deep dark green valley lay between them and the last pass.

29

The Valley

A path led down through the cool, dank air of the heavily wooded valley. Elenor brushed through shiny, dark leaves, stopping to rub her thumb over their mottled patterns. Thomas used his staff to knock a wild nut tree, and Elenor bent to gather nuts in her skirt. Without warning she saw something low and dark flash across the corner of her vision. She stood and turned, curious, unworried, and saw Thomas flying through the air. He landed with an inanimate thud.

"Climb a tree!" Martin shouted to Elenor. Not even aware of what she was doing, she grabbed a branch and scrambled up on it, scratching her face and arms, scattering nuts. There was a tiny space of time in which nothing happened. Elenor hung in the tree, breathing hard. Thomas lay on the ground. Martin stood over him, grasping a staff. Elenor kept her eyes on Thomas. He didn't move. Her throat hurt. Her ears rang in the silence; he seemed to have stopped breathing. Her breath made a tearing sound.

There was a rustling in the trees and the beast ran out again, charging Martin, a blur of black bristle, sharp tusks, and tiny, evil eyes. Martin met its charge with a crack of his staff. The beast barely wavered. It disappeared with a clatter into the underbrush on the other side of the clearing.

"Hurry, lass, we have to move him," said Martin. It was strange to hear Martin's voice, jolting the world back to normal, all except for Thomas. Elenor's legs barely held her when she landed on the ground. Thomas looked broken, like a doll a child has thrown in a tantrum. As motionless as in a deep sleep, but the angles were wrong.

"You'll be needing to drag him over my back," said Martin, falling on all fours. Elenor tugged on Thomas' inert body, pulled finally with all her strength, though she was terrified she would hurt him more, that he would die under her hands. She held him high enough that Martin was able to crawl under, scooping Thomas onto his back. Thomas' head flopped to one side. Elenor put her hand on his neck, covering it, because it looked pitifully vulnerable. She felt a faint pulse.

Martin struggled to keep Thomas off the ground and lurched through the forest blindly. Elenor went ahead of him, finding a path, holding branches away, fearing at every moment another rustling of the underbrush.

By late afternoon they had cleared the woods and were climbing another steep hillside. On the path, a miracle in this wildness, was a shrine. It bore an arrow and one word carved in stone: MISERICORDIA. *Mercy,* thought Elenor. *God's mercy, and people's. Mercy of the heart.* There would be nuns there, to help.

Elenor and Martin, half carrying, half dragging Thomas between them, stumbled uphill toward the clear blue air of the pass, where they could see the cross again.

Every second felt to Elenor precious and vivid as a jewel: the small painful rocks underfoot, the strong evening sun that lit huge gray clouds, the golden light that bathed the boulders, and the small white house that perched among them, so far above, always so far away, yet solid, reassuring, and serene. The path was often too narrow to go abreast: they inched sideways. The path broadened and Elenor was glad because then Martin shifted Thomas down from his back and shared the weight with her again. Thomas was still alive. She could feel a pulse where her hand grasped his wrist, a faint heartbeat where his armpit fit over her shoulder.

For weeks she had been turning questions in her mind, not thinking about them directly, but pondering through her stillness and drawing. Now she knew the answer, and it no longer seemed important. She would go back to Ramsay. She would do her part in the world in that place and with those people. If Thomas died, she would go alone. If she must, she could and would go alone.

Most of all, she wanted Thomas to live. To have time for work and stories, pine needles, children. She wanted Thomas to have his life. She wanted to live hers with him.

They kept climbing, struggling on, taking him to whatever help they could find.

30

Misericordia

T homas felt and heard nothing for a long time. He was in a deep sleep, soft as brown velvet. Whenever his mind began to awake, it bumped against some harshness and quickly retreated to nothingness. Much later there were dreams, or perhaps memories, from further back than he had ever remembered. The feeling of being rocked, a warm, sweet smell, a gentle crooning. He was neither big nor small, nor did he have a name. His life was like a candle flame in the darkness, without association.

Elenor was allowed to stay by his bedside. The nuns kept the ward clean, the walls whitewashed, the dirt floor swept. Sun streamed in the window. A Sister picked wild nasturtiums and set them in a jar on the sill. Elenor lost all sense of time, absorbing the brilliant reds and yellows of those small flowers and the strong blue of the sky.

Thomas shared a bed with an old pilgrim who

was near death. Elenor helped the Sisters wash the sheets outside in a tub and hang them on lines to flap in the wind and sun.

Thomas remained inert, sightless. He breathed, and sometimes his mouth twitched in his sleep.

"An angel is telling him jokes," said Sister Rosa, tucking a blanket around him.

Coming in one morning with clean sun-warmed sheets, Elenor thought he might be dead, he looked so calm and peaceful. Sorrowfully, she put her head on his chest. She heard his heart, still beating.

Martin slept for two full days. When he woke up, the nuns fed him and sent him down to the valley to get new thatch for the roof, a long climb down and back. He lived in the present, running his hand over the lichen that clung to the boulders, noticing the sharp smell of crushed wildflowers. The course of his own life hung in the balance along with Thomas'. If Thomas died, he would do what he could to help Elenor, whom he had grown to love and respect. But he loved Thomas, too, and did not think ahead. If Thomas lived, he would go back to Scotland, and one day they might fight each other across the border.

Martin lived in the present, looking for the house where he was to ask for thatch.

* * *

Thomas' bedmate died and was buried on the rocky hillside, almost within view of Santiago. A priest came up the mountain to say the prayers. He brought with him parchments, dispensations.

"If you are unable to continue on your pilgrimage, yet it is completed in the eyes of our Lord Jesus, of his Blessed Mother, of Saint James, and of the Holy Catholic Church."

The priest read this aloud, then offered the parchment to Elenor, for Thomas. It seemed evident to her that Thomas had made his pilgrimage, but she took the parchment in case it would be of comfort to someone back home.

The next day, Thomas woke up. It began with a stirring in his feet, flashes of light, pain, and nausea. There was a sense of fighting toward something not altogether pleasant. Was it the Garden of Eden? Was he passing through the wall of fire? He rested and drifted back toward sleep, toward kindly death. A hand touched his forehead, very gently, but it hurt because it made demands. It was the touch of a person, a person in need of response. To recognize the presence of a person required separating himself from simple existence. He could no longer be just a part of the web of life, like a plant or stone. He had to become human again, with the double burden of loneliness and responsibility.

Thomas took on life reluctantly. He dragged his spirit together and made the long journey away from the security of death, back to the edge of consciousness. Finally he opened his eyes and, when he did, saw Elenor. She had turned her head and was looking out the window. The clear mountain light brightened her face, which looked small, lonely, and very strong. For Thomas it was like looking in a mirror with no surface, into another soul in the same pool as his own. Others were there, too, all the others. He kept his eyes on her until she looked down at him. Then he took a deep breath that made his body come alive in all its painful, wracked dimensions, and he was glad even to feel pain, because he was no longer propelled by duty, but pulled forward by beautiful, desirable life.

Thomas recovered quickly, and the nuns loved him. His body, once he had made the decision to live, began busily to heal itself, ribs reknitting, lungs filling out to hold air again, the headaches fewer and less intense every day.

Martin and Sister Rosa made him crutches, the old Sister deftly peeling branches, trimming sticks, Martin fastening them together and trying them for size. Smell and taste came back to Thomas. "Pine," he said, sniffing his crutches.

"Walk beside him," said Sister Rosa. "You must be there to catch him. My baby is still so weak."

"Walk, old baby," Martin ordered, "or you'll na' have a fishy in your little dishy."

Martin and Elenor walked with him, ready to lunge and catch him.

Alone with Thomas one day, Elenor showed him the parchment.

"We could consider the pilgrimage done, the priest said."

"What do you think?" asked Thomas.

"I think I should go alone to Santiago and take the sins. Then I will come back and meet you here and we will travel home when you are able."

Thomas took her hand. He turned it over and looked at it as if he had never seen it before. He traced the blue veins on the inside of her wrist.

"Would you marry Martin?" he asked at last.

She was surprised by the question. "It would be possible," she answered. "We could make it work. But I would rather marry you, if you agree."

"I agree," he said, and kissed her wrist. "Wait with me, Nora." He got up painfully and put an arm over her shoulder, and together they covered the few yards to the door of the house.

* * *

What Martin saw now between Thomas and Nora made him lonesome. He feared for them on the steep mountain, but he needed to leave, to find his happy, single self.

"We'll meet in Santiago," he said. "And if not, I'll come to see you in England, Thomas. We'll toss the cawber together."

To Nora, all he could say was, "Take care of him, missy."

At the bend of the road he had to speak sternly to Greatheart to send him back to Nora.

31

Martin's Wait

artin dawdled all the way down the mountain, filling his ears with the rustling of leaves far up in the trees, breathing the pine wind, chewing sap beads, eating berries, easing hunger and loneliness, chasing tunes that were just around the corners of his mind. Some days later, he sat on a stone at the edge of the river at Lavacol, laughing deep inside at the pilgrims washing there, and wondering if a song could ever be dreamed up that would do justice to the jubilant scene before him. Everywhere people were throwing off their clothes, pouring water over their heads, splashing, shouting, and singing. On the bank of the river pilgrims spread their rags to dry in the sun or sat in companionable pairs, picking through each other's hair for lice, while some who were through washing knelt praying, tears of joy running down their faces. This was the last chance to clean up body and soul before approaching the holy city.

Martin was cleaner than he'd ever been, yet still he dawdled.

"Pray and delouse here," the priest had told him in four languages, "or you don't get into Santiago."

Did he want to get into Santiago? He thought of Elenor, flat on her back, feet crossed, staring into the throat of a morning glory. "I don't care if I never get home." Getting to Santiago seemed practice for dying, the only practice one got. The end of the pilgrimage, the beautiful parade. Martin watched the pilgrims fondly. Almost all of them were crazy, restless people like himself. Almost all of them, now, were ecstatic, ready to complete their pilgrimage, ready to go home. Did it mean that each had discovered purpose? Or that they didn't need purpose, that appreciation of life was enough? Did it mean that, when their time came to die, they would die graciously, willingly, knowingly?

Close to Martin, two friars were splashing each other; the water in the air caught the sun in a rainbow flash.

A priest stood in the water with his cassock tucked in his belt, revealing strong, hairy legs. Martin stared at him, wondering why he looked so familiar, and then realized he had seen a mural of this man as Saint Christopher in a wayside church somewhere back on the sunny plains. Back when they were all together. The priest was looking at Martin, scowling. Martin grinned at him.

He stayed at Lavacol because he loved it, and also because, before he made the last part of the pilgrimage, he wanted to know that Elenor and Thomas would make it, too. He knew it was right that he had left the mountain. He did not want to join their company again. He wanted to hover like a butterfly or a guardian angel. He wanted to know that they were well.

His toes were shriveling up from being in the water so long. He stared at them, wondering if there was any connection between the words "shriveled" and "shriven." Perhaps he should ask the priest. . . .

"Martino! *Ragazzo!*" His reverie was broken; he turned, along with everyone else on the bank. There was the *brigata*, and Melinda, too, a sight to make the lame leap with joy. Bea led the pack, her arms outstretched, her eyes sparkling. They all had their skirts tucked up the way they wore them for washing. Martin's heart turned a flip. Bea grabbed one of his hands and Gisella the other, and they dragged him into the water. Bea used Martin's hat to baptize first him, then each of the other girls, chanting joyfully in Italian while the priest looked on. When they were all washed and Martin's feet were blue with cold, they asked him for a blessing.

"Wait!" Martin protested, as the women dragged him away from Lavacol. "I haven't found the meaning of life." But Martin climbed to Santiago with the *brigata*.

They made the pilgrimage properly. They spent long hours gazing at the sculptured prophets of the Portico de la Gloria: wise and weary Moses; humble Isaiah deferring with a shrug to some opinion of Moses'; young Daniel, with his restless dancing feet, telling a funny story to stern, sad Jeremiah, whose burden was to bear bad tidings. They touched their foreheads three times to the carved curly head of Maestro Mateo, the sculptor, whose self-likeness knelt humbly in the church vestibule, since tradition held that this would make a person wise. Martin found the center of the cathedral and came for mass every day. He knelt before the body of Saint James, down in the crypt, and looked among the heaps of tokens and written prayers and petitions for the leather pouch Elenor had shown him, in which her priest, Gregory, had sewn the sins of their people, of Thornham and Ramsay. He gave to the beggars at the doors of the cathedral. He bought a scallop shell for his hat.

Days went by and the *brigata* was ready to set out for home. Martin hocked his knife to buy souvenir trinkets for them. They cried over leaving him, over leaving Santiago, over leaving without seeing Thomas and Nora again. They hugged him for everyone. He walked back down as far as Lavacol with them, glad when Bea finally took him by the shoulders and turned him around and shoved him forcefully back toward Santiago.

He scanned the faces in the street, thought he saw Elenor and Thomas, was elated then disappointed again and again. Blast their silly pilgrim hearts! Why did they all dress alike? He checked the hospice every day, questioning the harrassed Brothers who tried to minister to hordes of transients. He tried drawing pictures as he had watched Elenor do; she could capture a person's presence in a few lines. Martin could manage a fair portrait of Greatheart, but his people were lucky to get two eyes, two ears, and a nose. He scouted the dormitories, turned in the street at the barking of a dog, and hung about the door of the refectory to watch the pilgrims going in and coming out. He was ready to give it up, when one day a Brother at the cathedral hospice showed him a well-thumbed letter. "Is this the man you're always asking after?" said the friar, holding his grimy thumbnail under Thomas' name.

Martin thanked him and searched the outside of the packet for clues. It had been sent by a series of messengers. It appeared to have come from Ramsay. It was addressed to Thomas of Thornham, Elenor of Ramsay, Friends, In care of the Brothers in Christ, Pilgrim Hostelry, Santiago de Compostela.

Martin looked at the Brother. They broke the seal together, and helped each other with the reading. The letter said,

To his beloved and worthy friends Elenor, Thomas:
   Gregory, Brother in Christ, sends his greeting, his prayers, and his love.

   With sorrow I write the news that our friend Sir Robert, having met with a hunting accident shortly after your departure, is much weakened, though he still lives in hope of seeing you again. Each of you is missed and needed, now even more than on the morning you left. Many send questions, love, and most of all wishes that, relieved of our sins, you will speed home to us. I would eagerly prolong even this conversation with you, as it brings your faces across land and sea and keeps them lively by our hearth side. Know that on your return there will be swimming in the river and feasting on the green. If there is sorrow, there will also be joy and work of every kind. God's blessing on each of you.

   Your devoted friend, priest, and servant,
                                                        Gregory

"Brother, advise me," said Martin.

"Come," said the friar. He led Martin to a formal, empty cell with two wooden benches.

"How may I advise you?" he asked, when they were seated.

"My friends," said Martin, "to whom this letter is addressed, were at the Casa de Misericordia in Cebrera when I last saw them, recovering from a mishap. They may be making their way toward Compostela now."

"The snow will soon be flying in Cebrera, blocking the pass," said the Brother. "They have a dog," he added.

"Yes, Brother," said Martin, warming to this self-effacing man who remembered his drawings.

"It is, I believe, a three-legged dog," said the Brother.

Martin flushed. "Only in the picture, Brother."

"Will you return overland or by sea?"

Martin froze.

"To return overland, it is too late until spring. To return by sea, you must book passage now. Your courage is low? Pray with me."

With the Brother's help, Martin wrote a note, copied it ten times, and tacked these carefully written messages to the posts that stood for that purpose in the entry of the taverns and hostelries. The message read simply,

Thomas, Nora,

    Meet me under the Portico de la Gloria on All Saints' Eve. I have a letter for you.

Martin

That gave him a full fortnight to go find a ship.

32

The Ramsay Scallop

Up on the mountaintop, Thomas had lost all sense of urgency. The days flowed by and he was healing. There were still creaks and pops and sharp pains in his chest when he breathed in deeply, but these were less alarming every day. The broken bones in both legs were gradually knitting together, and feeling was creeping back into his toes.

Elenor's days began with mass and ended with vespers, filled with work in the sun and wind: laundry, scrubbing, lifting and moving the sick, gardening. *I could be a nun,* she realized one morning, as she knelt in the small bare chapel, seeing the golden nasturtiums glowing against the gray stone altar, listening to the hoarse voices of the Sisters of Misericordia singing the Ave Maria. She was happy working with these Sisters day in and day out. There was pleasure even in wringing out the heavy sheets when Sister Rosa was at the other end, and there was joy in taking these same sheets down sweet-smelling from the line and smoothing them onto the beds in the clean-swept ward. The word "nun," which had seemed so drab to her, now made her think of Sister Maria-Luz, jumping emphatically on the shovel as she dug the grave for the old dead pilgrim, shouting as clumps of dirt flew down the mountainside. She wanted to tell Father Gregory.

She could be a nun, but she wouldn't be one, not soon. Soon, and she hoped it would be for a long while, she was to be a married woman. Six months earlier, she had imagined the married Elenor as flat and finished as a queen on a playing card. Now the prospect amazed and dizzied her. Her heart pounded in her ribs as she swayed on her knees just thinking about it. She felt as if she were perched on the edge of a cliff, about to leap off and hoping it would turn out she could fly.

From the secure vantage of the Sisters of Misericordia, marriage seemed an absurdly complicated way of life. She understood why the Church required celibacy of its priests and nuns, now that she faced the double life of a person bound by sacrament to another. She would have love and companionship and encouragement and would give these, too. At the same time, she would be living her own life, trying to act and think for herself no matter what Thomas thought. She would have to accept that he would do things, believe things she didn't agree with. She would feel his doubts as keenly as if they were her own, and be helpless to fix them.

She was certain that Thomas would not try to lock her in the henhouse.

Don't go out walking at night, now," warned Sister Rosa. "One fall, and we'll have you two here until Easter."

Elenor didn't think that Sister Rosa would mind having them stay, she had taken such a liking to Thomas. But winter was coming on, and if they were to leave, it would have to be before snow fell in the pass. Thomas was getting stronger; they took walks every day. He managed his crutches well, even among the rocks. He couldn't do without them yet.

They stopped in the courtyard one night after compline, leaning against the low stone wall and looking at the stars, which swung low and bright in the clear, deep sky.

"I can hear them humming," said Thomas.

"Dancing and humming. They know ..."

"What?"

"What to do," said Elenor uncertainly.

Thomas rested his crutches against the wall and sat on the stones, glad to give his arms a rest. Someone blew out the candles in the chapel. Sisters passed by murmuring good-night on their way to bed. Soon the only sounds were the blowing of the wind, the night conversation of sheep, the humming of the stars.

Elenor stood close by Thomas, her head on a level with his, wanting to be near, wanting to hear his voice. Thomas watched the stars.

"They're calling us home, Nora."

"How can you tell?"

"Look how they each dance so grandly, in a big circle, and always come back to their right place."

Elenor thought of what she'd said to Pierre when he had asked what she was in the world to do: "I am to take my parents' place, and help make our village good to live in."

"And we're to do the same? To come back to our right place?"

Thomas nodded. He cleared his throat, and laughter crept into his voice. "As Etienne would say, the celestial spheres are casting their influence upon us in hopes that we will—"

"Dance grandly home," Elenor finished for him.

Thomas nodded again, putting his hands on her shoulders and turning her gently toward him.

"We're still a long, long way from home," said Elenor, panicked into talking.

"We have each other. That's home."

Elenor gave up resisting, and as if in fact subject

to some cosmic pull, moved to stand between Thomas' knees as he sat there on the wall, and flung her arms around his neck as she had been longing to do.

"We could be married now," said Thomas, at length. Elenor was discovering the feel of the planes of his face and had trouble focusing on his words.

"Because of the dispensation?" she asked, and was surprised that her voice was the same. She drew back, and found this simple step as hard as fighting a tide or a strong wind. She even folded her arms across her chest.

"Yes," Thomas answered. What had she asked?

"I think we are married now, anyway," she said, not knowing she would.

"Yes."

"We can have a priest in Santiago read the prayers."

"All right."

"And Father Gregory can say them again when we get home."

"Nora, you are talking a lot now," he observed.

"I'm scared, Thomas. I don't know much about this."

"Neither do I, my very dear Nora, believe me. We'll learn."

"And, I think we have to respect the way the Sisters live, while we're here."

"Yes, Nora."

She looked at him and her eyes sparkled. "So maybe we had better leave soon."

The nuns did not come to wave good-bye to them. Elenor went to each one as she worked, embracing her and wishing her well; Sister Rosa as she smoothed boards in her workshop, Sister Maria-Luz as she scrubbed the floor of the ward, Sister Dolores at the laundry tub. Thomas was making his own rounds. They met at the top of the path, Thomas leaning on his crutches, Greatheart running on ahead.

They stood together at the top of the path, turned toward each other. The wind was blowing. Thomas had grown gaunt, and he had changed in other ways. A light seemed to shine through him. Elenor thought that the Sisters' careful and motherly nursing had taken away some pain, some doubt about himself that Thomas had carried for as long as she had known him. Elenor worried that the Sisters had given them so much, not only Thomas' very life, but his new and certain happiness, while they had given little in return. "I wish I could leave them something beautiful."

"They have everything that is beautiful," said Thomas, patting his chest, "inside."

She knew he was right. The Sisters lived in the confidence that their work accorded with God's will.

Their path met the Way at a river just below the city, at a place called Lavacol, because it was ordained that all pilgrims should stop there to wash before entering the city. A hairy priest was on hand to greet the pilgrims and enforce the ordinance. Thomas and Elenor, free of lice, thanks to the Sisters' good care, poured water on each other using their hats, dried off in the sun, were blessed, and then were showered again by Greatheart.

Then, for the very last section of the Way, they joined the throng of pilgrims and let themselves melt into the crowd.

The towers of the cathedral dominated the town; storks nested above the bells. Green moss crept over stone walls and slate roofs. A fine mist of rain, the rain of ships and seaports, danced in the air. The streets they passed through were jammed with the stands of souvenir vendors, sellers of scapulars and beads, of leaden figurines and vials of holy water, of scallop shells and every kind of religious trinket. Thomas looked at Elenor.

"Should we?"

Elenor just shook her head, laughing. The carnival atmosphere elated and amazed her. They were swept to the very steps of the cathedral before they knew what had happened, then under the lovely portico, and into the cool dark depths of the sanctuary. There they were suddenly funneled into a sort of walkway for pilgrims, which ran around the inner walls of the cathedral. The murmur of voices, thousands of them, rolling like surf around the cathedral, the stench of thousands of bodies pressed close together, overlaid by the sweet, heavy smell of incense, the incantations of the priests, the wavering lights of tapers, the painted statues that seemed to lurch overhead as she was hurried along combined to fill Elenor first with awe, then with panic. She had meant to stay close by Thomas, to protect him as best she could from the jostling crowd, but she was swept away, catching just a glimpse of him, still upright on his crutches, clutching the packet of sins under his arm, looking pale. Then she lost him. She could neither direct herself nor flee; the tide of bodies carried her. Elbows and shoulders pushed into her body from every side. She made herself as tall as possible. Desperately afraid of being trampled, she tried to keep her face up as one would above floodwaters. There was almost no weight on her feet, though she touched the stone floor now and then, pushing off, getting her bearings.

She prayed fervently now, but it was not a prayer for grace, nor did she remember Carla, or Mathilde, or Fra Pietro, or any of the people she had promised to pray for. Her prayer, if it was to Saint James at all, was to James the fisherman. It said, over and over, "Don't let me be crushed. Get me out of here alive. Keep Thomas on his feet."

She clung to a remembrance of the mountaintop, with its golden light, its peace and certainty. The stream of pilgrims flowed right around the cathedral, behind the altar, and back down the other side of the nave in an unending circuit. Finally Elenor was borne straight out the door, into the dazzling brightness of day, the cool touch of the rain. Not far away, Thomas' crutches were leaned up against the portal. Thomas stood, pale and bent over, his hands around the ankles of a stone saint, his forehead resting on the damp granite. Greatheart was at his feet. The sins were gone.

Elenor was so relieved to be out of the press of pilgrims and to see Thomas alive that she closed her eyes and lifted her face to the sky, breathing in the sea air and welcoming the misty rain on her face. She tried to think of home, to turn her thoughts toward Ramsay, since it was for Ramsay they had come, but England seemed so far away she could hardly imagine it. She thought of Father

Gregory and Carla sitting together before the fire, and wondered if they would laugh at her change of heart about Thomas.

When she opened her eyes, Thomas had turned toward her and was waiting for her, a feel-foolish grin covering a look of serious joy, his arms outstretched, brandishing a scallop shell in one hand.